Skin Deep

By

Marilyn Lee

This is a work of fiction. Names, characters, places, and incidents are products of the author's imagination or are used fictitiously and are not to be construed as real. Any resemblance to actual events, locales, organizations, or persons, living or dead, is entirely coincidental.

Skin Deep by Marilyn Lee

Red Rose™ Publishing
Publishing with a touch of Class! ™
The symbol of the Red Rose and Red Rose is a trademark of Red Rose™ Publishing

Red Rose™ Publishing
Copyright© 2007 Marilyn Lee
ISBN: 1-60435-965-X
ISBN: 978-1-60435-965-7
Cover Artist: Nikita Gordyn
Editor: Red Rose™ Publishing
Line Editor: Sherri Good

All rights reserved. No part of this book may be used or reproduced electronically or in print without written permission, except in the case of brief quotations embodied in reviews. Due to copyright laws you cannot trade, sell or give any ebooks away.
This is a work of fiction. All references to real places, people, or events are coincidental, and if not coincidental, are used fictitiously. All trademarks, service marks, registered trademarks, and registered service marks are the property of their respective owners and are used herein for identification purposes only.

Red Rose™ Publishing
www.redrosepublishing.com
Forestport, NY 13338

Thank you for purchasing a book from Red Rose™ Publishing where publishing comes with a touch of Class!

Chapter One

Jake

My mother, a beautiful, generous woman, often said beauty was only skin deep. Maybe so, but show me a man who doesn't prefer a beautiful woman to a plain one and I'll show you a blind man. Despite my mother's efforts, I'd never dated a female I didn't find drop dead gorgeous. Don't get me wrong. I have nothing against ordinary women. I've just never seen the need to date one—until I met Bree.

The moment I saw her, I knew I'd been had, and that I would be getting even. I also knew I had to go through with the date-no matter how much I wanted to pretend I was at the wrong apartment.

Before you think I'm some fickle knucklehead unable to see past appearances, I'll save you the trouble and admit that, like most males, I prefer a woman I spend time with to be at least pretty. Her being beautiful would be even better.

I preferred slender, petite, gorgeous women with green eyes, fair skin and long, flowing red hair. Bree's skin was dark and clear, her eyes were an ordinary brown, and she wore her dark hair short and natural. I guessed she was roughly five eight—hardly petite. There would be no swinging her up into my arms and carrying her off to bed after a night of wining and dining.

I could have dealt with Bree's other shortcomings—had she at least been pretty. Granted, she had a nice smile. Actually she had a fantastic smile that shown in her eyes. Even so, it would be a stretch to call her anything other than...almost cute. I don't mean to imply that she was thoroughly unattractive. She wasn't, but she bore no resemblance to my ideal woman.

"You must be Jake."

I blinked. Her voice was husky—in a surprisingly sexy way. Her great smile and intriguing voice wouldn't get her past first base with me.

"Jake? I'm Gabrielle Williams."

I swallowed hard, hoping no trace of the dismay I felt showed on my face. I might have managed that, but for the moment, I was literally speechless at the situation I'd allowed Lea to maneuver me into.

She offered her hand. "My friends call me Bree."

I smiled and shook her hand briefly. It was soft and warm, yet she had a firm handshake. "Jake Volmer."

She glanced briefly over her shoulder into her apartment. "Would you like to come in for a drink?"

"No." Realizing I'd spoken too quickly and decisively, I smiled again. "We have reservations. If you're ready, we should go."

She gave me a long, piercing look, sighed and then shook her head. "You don't need to do this."

"What do you mean?"

"I can see I'm not what you expected."

Now that was an understatement if ever I'd heard one. "What?"

"What did Lea say to get you here tonight?"

Lea was my sister-in-law who was forever complaining that I was too fickle when it came to women. She's a fine one to talk about fickleness, but I'd lost track of the number of times she'd told me that I wouldn't know a good woman if I fell over her. Why the hell had I allowed her to talk me into a blind date just to prove — what? What the hell was this date going to prove, except that even married to my younger brother, Ed, Lea could still manipulate me?

I knew Lea expected me to take one look at Bree and find a way to back out of the date. Then she could gloat and say I-told-you-so for the next year or so when we met at family functions. Well, hell would freeze over before I gave Lea that satisfaction.

I arched a brow and smiled down at Bree. "I'm not dating anyone, so Lea suggested we might enjoy spending an evening together."

"I can see that my appearance surprises you."

"I have no idea what you're talking about."

She nodded. "I think you do. You don't have to go through with this."

If she didn't want to go out with me, why had she allowed Lea to set up this date? Were she and Lea in this together? Were they both expecting me to back out? Then they were both going to be disappointed. I narrowed my gaze, wondering just how deeply she had plotted with Lea. How far was she prepared to go to make me look bad?

"Let's chalk this up to a mistake, Jake."

In her damned dreams. I shook my head. "Absolutely not. As I said, we have a reservation." I offered her my arm. "Are you ready?"

She hesitated for several moments before she turned that slow, enchanting smile of hers on me.

I stared down into her warm brown eyes and swallowed. Damn. That smile of hers was very nice.

She slipped her arm through mine. "If you're sure, I'm ready."

Looking down into her dark, alluring gaze, the only thing I was sure of was that I was no longer sure of much of anything. But hell would freeze over before I allowed her and Lea the satisfaction of my walking away. At the end of the evening, I was going to teach her a lesson that ensured she wouldn't conspire against another man.

"Great. So, let's go."

On the drive to the restaurant, the soft, seductive scent of her perfume made it difficult to concentrate on my newly formed game plan. I realized she was speaking and frowned. "I'm sorry. What did you say?"

She brushed her fingers against my right hand on the steering wheel. I felt a jolt of heat rushing up the back of my neck. What the hell was she doing touching me? I tightened my grip and clenched my jaw.

"Where are we were having dinner?"

"Lea said you liked French."

"I love French."

So Lea had been honest about something at least. "Great. I think you'll like the place I picked out."

"I'm sure I will."

I cast a quick glance at her smiling profile. Okay, so she wasn't pretty, she wasn't petite, her hair wasn't long and flowing and her skin wasn't creamy. Nevertheless, she was smooth and manipulative. I narrowed my gaze as she brushed her fingers against my hand again.

Why should a woman who bore no resemblance to my ideal lover have the ability to unnerve me? I suddenly realized I'd need to be very careful or she and Lea would make a fool out of me.

Our dinner conversation was a blur. I vaguely remembered watching her full, lush lips moving. A mouth that sexy was good for one thing—endless kissing.

The next day, all I could recall was the rush of heat along the back of my neck and the stirring in my cock each time I looked up from my plate and encountered her dark, bottomless gaze.

For all of Bree's seeming lack of beauty, I spent the night thinking of hot, sleazy, bang-her-until-she-walked-bow-legged sex. Imagining her naked with her knees bent and her dark legs spread wide in an open invitation, made my cock stir. She had large breasts, big legs, and a round ass I ached to see naked and glistening with my cum.

I can't explain how I went from dismay to full-blown lust in a matter of a few hours. By the time she suggested we should leave, all I could think about was crawling into bed with her and thrusting my cock between her dark thighs and into her cunt. Somehow, she had managed to get me as horny as hell with very little effort on her part. Still, I was sure after a few fucks, I'd shake off my inexplicable, temporary insanity.

The return trip to her apartment seemed to last forever. Aroused and horny, I longed to slide my hand under her dress, run my palm along her legs, between her thighs—not stopping until my fingers brushed against her pussy.

I wondered what it looked like. Surely a dark tangle of curls surrounded it. Or did she shave it? Personally, I prefer a woman with lots of pubic hair that almost obscures her slit. I like pressing the head of my cock against it, probing for her entrance. Then I love the feel of it brushing against me as I slowly push into her honey hole.

I'd know soon enough. Come hell or high water, I was going to be spending the next few hours with my cock buried as far up her pussy as I could get it. If I were lucky, I might even get to fuck her ass. I wouldn't be greedy. If push came to shove, I'd settle for vaginal sex.

Judging by her come-ons all night, I knew she wanted to spend the night fucking.

At her apartment door, when she placed her hand on my arm and smiled up at me, I leaned down for my first taste of her sensuous looking lips. Instead of leaning into me and lifting her chin, she deliberately turned her head. My lips brushed against her cheek.

What the hell. Did she plan to play hard to get?

I turned my head and sought her lips again.

She shook her head, whispered a very clear no and drew away from me.

I stared down at her, confused. "What's wrong?"

"Nothing's wrong. I had a nice time, but the evening is over."

I caressed her cheek. "It doesn't have to be."

"Yes, it does. Thanks for a nice evening. Goodbye, Jake."

I frowned. "Goodbye?"

"Yes. Goodbye."

"Why goodbye instead of good night?"

She hesitated and then spoke in a husky, breathless rush. "Even though I enjoyed tonight, I'm fairly certain you didn't."

Now that took some damn nerve to tell me what I had or hadn't enjoyed. Once the fog in my brain cleared enough for me to recall the evening, I doubted I'd recall having been bored. "Of course I enjoy—"

She shook her head firmly, her dark eyes glinting up at me. "Please don't make this worse by lying."

I narrowed my gaze. "Lying?"

"Yes. There's no need to pretend you enjoyed tonight. Goodbye."

"Wait a minute—"

"Goodbye," she said again and damned if the conniving hussy didn't step into her apartment and close the door firmly in my face.

I must have stood there for several minutes—in surprised shock. She'd been sending signals all night and then she closed the door in my face and left me with blue balls? What the hell did she expect me to do? Go home and take a cold shower? It was times like these when I most regretted the loss of Lea—the one woman who could bring me to my knees with but a flash of her bare cunt.

If you're wondering why a thirty-year-old up and coming engineer doesn't have a woman in his life, you can blame it on Lea and my unrelenting hunger for her. At our first meeting she took my breath away and ruined me for all other women. Then when I was madly in love with her, she kicked me out of her bed and went after my brother Ed.

After my experience with her, it was difficult to view women as anything but conniving hussies whose interest in a man's cock size was only overshadowed by their interest in the size of his bank balance.

Within the space of three months, my brother and I were both mad about Lea, but Ed had won a two million dollar jackpot. So which one of us do you think the little, faithless bitch reeled in?

Granted I owned a condo, drove a new luxury car every other year, and I had the potential to keep her in a very comfortable life-style in another year or so. Ed was already there, so I watched the woman with whom I was in big-time lust marry my little brother.

That was three years ago. During that time, although I'd had my share of dates, I hadn't met any woman capable of arousing my lust to the levels that Lea had. So I had an endless series of one-night stands—all while my lust for Lea grew.

Don't get me wrong. I didn't intend to betray Ed's trust by making a play for Lea. But the faithless bitch wanted it all—Ed's money and my cock. She did her best to keep me enslaved to my hunger for her.

The moment Ed's back was turned I could count on her hitching up her skirt to show an enticing expanse of slender, pale thigh. Hell, the shameless bitch often parted her legs to give me a long, enticing look at her bare pussy. She shaves her pubs and every time she flashed me and I saw her nether lips, I got an instant hard on. That's when I'd remember the many nights I'd spent buried balls deep in her tight cunt with her legs wrapped around me while she humped herself on my cock as if she were as addicted to it as I was to her pussy. I'd want her more than ever.

She enjoyed jerking my chain, seeing how close she could get me to sleeping with her. But no matter how much I wanted it, I swore I'd cut my balls off before I'd sleep with her now that she belonged to Ed. But standing outside Bree's door burning with lust and knowing Ed was away on a business trip, I allowed lustful thoughts to linger.

Instead of going home, I could drive to that big, suburban home Ed had bought her. I could strip her naked and fuck her all night in their big, brass bed. Or maybe I'd handcuff her to the bed and fuck her ass until she moaned with satisfied lust.

Halfway there, I came to my senses. I turned and went home. I stripped in my bedroom and headed into my bathroom. As I stood under the cold shower, I cursed Lea and her damned accomplice Bree for my sexual frustration. I also plotted revenge.

Life is too short to spend it in pursuit of vengeance, but I was so pissed, I knew my life would be miserable until I got even. Since Lea was Ed's wife, there was only so much I could do or say to her. That left her partner in crime Bree to pay for their treachery.

I masturbated in the shower before I dried off and went to bed.

As I lay sleepless and aroused, I discarded plan after plan before finally settling on one I felt would give me a measure of revenge. While I had no desire to cause Bree physical injury, I was determined to fuck her senseless and to teach her not to stick her nose in family affairs.

I was still horny—even after coming in the shower. I fell asleep after what felt like hours of frustration. The next morning, I was tired, but determined. As I waited for my coffee to perk, I went online, found a local florist and ordered an elaborate bouquet of flowers.

I had settled into my recliner in the living room and was sipping my coffee, biding my time until I judged it wouldn't be too early to call Bree when my phone rang. I glanced at the caller ID screen before smiling and answering.

"Hey."

"Hey yourself. So? How did it go?"

My smile turned into a grin. It was just like Jess to decide I was taking too long to fill her in on my date and call to get the details before I was ready to share them. Not that I minded. Much to her husband's displeasure, Jess and I were as close as we'd been in college. Granted ours was a strange friendship, but it had stood the test of time.

Most of our friends and some of the women in my life had come to understand that the only thing I shared with the Angela Bassett look-alike was friendship. Our relationship hadn't always been platonic. The sexual part of our relationship ended near the end of our junior year of college. Our friendship had survived.

I shook my head, forcing myself to concentrate on Jess's voice. "It didn't."

"Tell me about it," she invited.

"Where's Malik?" I knew he wouldn't take kindly to what he'd call my monopolizing her on a Saturday morning.

"He's not here."

"He's not?" He often used the excuse of their spending time together on the weekend as an excuse to make it as difficult for us to see each other as possible. "Is everything okay?"

"Yes."

I noted the hesitancy in her voice. I frowned. "Are you sure?"

She spoke after another pulse. "Yes. Now give."

I attempted to keep my voice neutral and made no mention of my plans for revenge as I shared the details of my date with Bree.

"Closed the door in your face?"

I frowned. She sounded amused.

"You wouldn't be losing some of that blue-eyed charm of yours, would you?"

I wasn't in the mood for jokes. At six-three with a muscular body I worked to keep toned, said blue eyes and what I'd been told by more than one lover was a big, hard, sweet, hot, cock, I'd never had any problems landing and keeping the woman of my choice—until Lea.

I shrugged. "It doesn't matter because she's not my type."

"Then why are you sending her flowers and planning to call her? What are you up to, Jake?"

I suppressed a sigh, wondering when I'd learn not to tell Jess too much. Along with Chuck, who I'd known since junior high, Jess was one of my closest friends. When it came to uncovering things I'd rather not admit, Jess had no peer. She was fond of saying she knew me like she knew the back of her hand.

"Don't go trying to get psychic on me, Jess. I'm not planning anything."

"Then why send her flowers? That will only encourage her to think you want to see her again."

Oh, I was hell bent on seeing her again—just long enough to get her into the sack a few times. Then I'd move on. And I'd sure as hell know better than to allow Lea to set me up on a blind date again. "I don't have any other prospects at the moment."

"So you'll risk leading her on and then dropping her when someone who is your type comes along? That's not like you, Jake."

"Look, you're making too much of this. I'm talking about a few dates at most. I promise I won't hurt her."

"You'd better not or you'll have to deal with me," she warned.

"You don't know her, do you?"

"No but when dating a good-looking, sweet-talking white man looking to break hearts, black women have to stick together."

"What? Break your...Our breakup was mutual. I didn't break your heart." I frowned. "Did I? I mean...You said—"

"Relax, Jake. You didn't break my heart, but only because I was careful not to fall in love with you. When a black woman falls for a white man...it opens up all kinds of potential problems for her."

I wasn't in the mood to discuss the social ramifications of interracial dating. I didn't want nor need anyone telling me who I could or should date. "She's a big girl, Jess. I'm not going to be seeing her long enough for either one of us to get hurt."

"Look, Jake, I know you won't hurt her intentionally, but you're a big, good-looking man. If you're not careful she could start to feel more for you than she should within a short time. So just be careful with her heart."

I had zero interest in her heart. Her pussy was another story. "I will."

"Okay."

"Okay. Now. You want to tell me what's wrong between you and Malik?"

As before there was a noticeable pause before she answered. "Nothing's wrong. Look. I have to go. "

"Jess."

"What?"

"If you need to talk, I'm always here for you," I said quietly.

Her voice had softened when she spoke again. "I know. Thanks for your concern, but Malik and I will work things out."

So there was something to work out. I shook my head. Malik was a bigger fool than I thought he was if he let Jess slip away from him. "You want to talk now?"

"No. Now...I just need to...I have to get a move on. I'll talk to you in a few days."

"Okay, but if you need anything—"

"I know. Thanks, Jake." She made a kissing sound and hung up.

Chapter Two

Bree

I was surprised and delighted when the beautiful bouquet arrived late Saturday morning. Eight months earlier, Darren, the regional sales manager I'd been dating for nearly a year, had accepted a promotion which necessitated a cross-country move to California.

He'd made noises about our having a long distance relationship. Although tempted to agree, I knew he'd lose interest in me once he worked in L.A. with all those svelte, hard-bodied women with tanned skin and long, flowing hair. He'd offered to fly back to Philly for a long weekend a few times. I had reluctantly decided a clean break was best.

When he'd finally accepted our relationship was over, he'd sent me a goodbye bouquet four months earlier. The flowers brought back pleasant memories of the intimate relationship we'd shared. I smiled at his persistence. Maybe I needed to rethink my position on long distance relationships.

If he still wanted me after eight months, his feelings must run deeply. It was flattering that those L.A. ladies hadn't changed his mind. My main reason for ending our relationship had been my fear that he wouldn't be able to remain faithful. I can forgive a lot when I'm in love, but I draw the line at infidelity. A renewed relationship with Darren would drive thoughts of the handsome, sexy Jake from my thoughts.

My pleasure turned to amazement as I read the card that accompanied the flowers.

May I call you?

Jake V.

Recovering from the faint disappointment that the flowers weren't from Darren, I sat staring at the card. Why had Jake sent them? Despite his denials, I'd seen his initial surprise when we met the previous night. He'd spent most of the evening staring at me with a bemused look on his face. His half-hearted attempt to get me into bed notwithstanding, I was certain he was relieved when the evening was over.

So why send flowers? Why pretend he wanted to see me again? Had Lea somehow conned him into it again? Lea and I had shared a couple of lunches and an occasional quick in-office dinner when we worked late. We were a little more than just cordial with each other, but far less than true friends who shared each other's innermost confidences. She knew I'd ended my relationship with Darren, but not why.

Sympathy had probably motivated her to set me up with Jake. We needed to talk. I put a load of clothes in the washer before I called her.

She listened in silence for several moments before she spoke. "He sent you flowers? Jake sent you flowers?"

"Yes."

"He's not a flower sending guy. He actually said he wanted to see you again?"

The blatant surprise in her voice annoyed me. If she found his wanting to see me again such a surprise, why had she arranged a blind date for us in the first place?

"Why do you sound so surprised?"

In the two years Lea and I had been accountants at a large car dealership, I'd come to appreciate her quick wit.

"Surprised? I knew you two would hit it off. I just didn't realize the first date would go so...well. When are you seeing him again?"

Recalling how my heart raced when he'd attempted to kiss me, I sighed. I was lonely. I wanted a man in my life. But I wanted one who wanted to be there because he found me attractive, not because Lea had somehow corralled him into it. If Darren was still interested, I wanted him there-even if it were only on a part-time, long-distance basis.

"I'm not."

"So when he calls and asks you out again, you're going to say no?"

"Yes."

"Oh."

Why did she sound so pleased? Why had she arranged our blind date? Even if she had felt sorry for me, Jake clearly didn't require help getting a date. She clearly hadn't expected him to want to see me again. Sometimes she was less than cordial. As my grandmother used to say, still waters ran deep. Taking Lea at face value was probably a mistake.

"Well, it's getting late and I still have tons of things to get done today. I'll see you on Monday, Lea."

"Great. Will you do me a favor?"

"If I can."

"Oh you can. Just let Jake down gently."

She definitely had something up her sleeve. But what? "Sure will. Bye."

I hung up and then jumped when the phone immediately rang. I glanced at the caller ID. I answered after a brief hesitation. "Hello?"

"Hi Bree? This is Jake Volmer."

I moistened my lips. "Hi. Ah...thanks for the flowers. They're lovely."

"You're welcome."

"They were as surprising as is this call."

"I'm not sure why the flowers or this call would come as a surprise."

"Lea said you weren't the flower sending kind of guy."

There was a brief, almost palpable silence before he spoke in a terse voice. "You've discussed me with Lea?"

I frowned, not sure what to make of his tone or the implication of the question. I instinctively knew admitting we'd 'discussed' him would be unwise. "We didn't discuss you, but naturally she wanted to know how our date went."

"How did it go?"

"Not well."

"Why not?"

"I'm sure I'm not your type."

My grandmother used to warn me to be careful what I wished for in case I got it. That happened when he spoke again. "No, you're not."

His confirmation of what I already knew shouldn't hurt. Maybe hurt was too strong a word. It stung. I swallowed hard. "Well...at least you've decided to be honest. Now that we've cleared the air, I'll—"

"You didn't let me finish."

"I think you've said enough."

"No. I haven't."

He would not get another chance to sting me. "Then let me put it another way. You've said as much as I want to hear."

"Don't misunderstand me, Bree—"

"I haven't misunderstood a thing about you from the moment we met."

"What the hell's that's supposed to mean?"

"Figure it out."

"I'd rather finish my sentence."

"Make it quick."

"It's true you're not my type, but—"

I sucked in an angry breath. "There's no need to repeat yourself."

"Before you get angry—"

"I'm not angry."

"Yeah. Right. Before you get angry enough to hang up on me—"

"Hanging up on people is rude."

"So is slamming doors in their faces," he shot back.

"I didn't slam the door in your face. I said goodbye. It's not my fault if you don't understand English and can't take a damned hint."

There was a brief, tense silence. Then he laughed.

I was not amused. "What's so funny?"

"It's very early in our relationship to have this lover's quarrel."

"We're not quarreling. We're having a spirited discussion and we are *not* lovers."

"So I noticed—when you slammed the door in my face."

I compressed my lips. "I'm a little busy at the moment so—"

"So if I'm not quick, you'll hang up on me?"

He sounded amused and that annoyed the hell out of me. "You were saying?"

"I was saying opposites attract."

That was another one of my grandmother's favorite sayings. "Not in our case."

When he replied his voice no longer held that annoying, amused tone that grated on my nerves. "Do you have any reason to doubt my word?"

"No, but—"

"Then please don't presume to know who or what I find attractive. Now, what are your plans for tonight?"

"I don't actually have any, but—"

"Great. I'll pick you up at six. Dress casually."

"Hey. Wait a minute."

"You sound frantic, Bree. Are you afraid I'm about to hang up on you?"

There was that damned amusement again. "Were you?"

"Yes, so make it quick. You're not the only one who has things to do today."

"What? Look...If you think you can..." I paused and took a deep, calming breath. "I haven't said I'm going out with you."

"But you will."

His looks probably accounted for the confidence I heard in his voice. "I—"

"I'll be there at six. Get ready because here it comes."

"What?"

"I'm hanging up now. Bye."

He hung up.

I put down the phone. It was foolish to go out with Jake when I'd all but decided to renew my relationship with Darren—assuming he was still interested. That was a big assumption since I had not heard from him in four months.

For reasons of his own, the sexy Jake wanted to see me again. I closed my eyes, remembering the feel of his body against mine and the smell of his subtle cologne. His lips had felt nice against my cheek. What would they feel like against my mouth...moving over my parted lips? I swallowed slowly, feeling a rush of heat warming my cheeks. Maybe this time I'd let him kiss my lips. I opened my eyes.

That assumed I was going out with him. Who was I kidding? I was going out with him and in all likelihood, when he attempted to kiss me I was going to kiss him back. I wasn't prepared to go any further than kissing on a second date. Still a kiss shared with the right partner could be so much more than a kiss.

Chapter Three

Jake

I felt restless after talking to Bree. I knew if I had any sense, I'd call her back, cancel the date she didn't seem to want anyway, and never look in her direction again. Hadn't she practically admitted she was in cahoots with Lea? Why the hell should I allow Lea to use Bree to continue to push my buttons? What kind of woman was Bree that she'd allow Lea to use her to get to me? What the hell had I ever done to Bree?

Despite the dictates of commonsense, I spent far too much time wondering if Bree kissed on the second date. Actually, I hoped she did a lot more than kiss. The sooner I got her into bed, the sooner I could move on. She was clearly bad news to me. I was damned determined to see her again-whether she wanted to see me again or not.

After admitting I wouldn't get anything accomplished that day, I went to the gym to work out. I returned home to shower and dress for my date with Bree. Bree. What the hell kind of name was that anyway? How stupid was I to see her again knowing she was out to get me?

I needed to talk to someone to help clear my head. If I called Chuck, as soon as he learned Bree wasn't a knockout, he'd look at me like I'd lost my mind and ask me why I was even interested. If I called Jess, I might be making things worse between her and Malik. Besides, she'd just give me a third degree questioning I wasn't in the mood for. If I called Mom, she'd start making wedding plans.

Shaking my head, I opened my condo door and froze. Lea sat in a chair opposite the front door. Have I told you how absolutely gorgeous she is? She has the face of an angel and a petite, slender body made for sin. She has mounds of beautiful red-gold hair that cascades over her slender shoulders and sexy green eyes that hint she wants some lucky man to fuck her all night long.

I closed the door and stood staring at her. She smiled and slowly parted her legs, giving me an enticing view of her bare, shaved pussy.

I swallowed hard—and willed myself not to rise to the bait. "How did you get in?" To my annoyance, the question sounded more needy than demanding.

She spread her legs wider and held up a set of keys. "Eddy keeps your spare keys in his nightstand drawer. As you know, he's out of town."

I forced myself to meet her gaze. "That doesn't explain what you're doing here."

"I know your date with Bree went badly so you must be horny as hell. So am I." As she rose, the loose-fitting white dress she wore opened.

She's lovely. She has small, pert breasts, a flat stomach, slender, but shapely legs, and that addictive bare pussy I so loved to fuck. I felt as if I had to struggle to drag air into my lungs. I shook my head, even as my cock tightened against my thigh.

She took off the dress and tossed it aside, which left her standing in front of me in nothing but a pair of stiletto heels and sheer black stockings that clung to her lower thighs.

Noting my reaction, she smiled and massaged her hot, tight pussy. "I need a big, hard cock shoved deep into my wet kitty."

I resisted the urge to rush across the room and ravish her. "Well you're not getting any of mine."

"We'll see about that." She crossed the room to stand inches from me, with her head tilted back so she could look up into my eyes. "You know you and Eddy look so much alike, you and I can fuck without a condom."

I stared down at her. We'd never had sex without protection. Now that the bitch belonged to Eddy she wanted unprotected sex?

She smiled up at me, licking her lips suggestively. "The best part is, when you get me pregnant, no one will know it's your baby instead of Eddy's. You can fuck me as long as you want, shoot a river of cum into my pussy and get me pregnant. Then I'll have nearly everything I want—including your baby."

"If you want a baby, you can damn well wait for him to knock you up."

She shook her head, rubbing her pussy. "Oh no. I want you to fuck me, Jake—right now."

"It's not going to happen. Put your damned dress back on and get the hell out of here. I have a date."

Her pink lips curved upward. "With Bree?" She laughed. "Don't expect me to believe you'd rather be spending a platonic night with her than spending the night in my sweet kitty." She dipped several fingers between her legs, pumped them into her cunt. She got them wet before she pressed her fingers against my lips. "Taste my pussy juice and then tell me you don't want me."

The taste and scent of her aroused cunt made me rock hard—as it always had. Despite myself, I greedily licked the sweet moisture from her fingers.

Smiling, she took one of my hands and pressed it between her legs. I couldn't stop myself from stroking my fingers into her hot, tight box. She moaned softly and started fucking herself on my fingers. "Oh yes. Yes."

I took a deep breath and pulled my fingers from her cunt. "We can't do this. He's my brother and your husband. Don't you care anything about him?"

She arched a brow and pushed my fingers back into her cunt. "Of course I care about him. I know you think it's just the money, but it's not."

"If you care about him, what the fuck are you doing here trying to seduce me?"

She closed her thighs over my hand and rotated her slender hips. Moaning softly, she rode my thrusting fingers. "He's a sweet man who loves me, but after developing a taste for your cock, his just isn't big, thick, or hard enough." She thrust a hand down my sweats, into my briefs.

I shuddered as she cupped my fully erect cock. "Oh Jake. I can't tell you how many nights I closed my eyes when he fucked me and pretended his cock was yours. I need this monster of yours thrusting so deep inside me I can almost feel you moving under the skin of my belly. I want this cock and I want it now."

I struggled with the lust, which threatened to override my concern and love for Eddy. As I did, I continued to finger fuck her. She started to jerk me off.

Within minutes, I was lost in a world of lust. I closed my eyes and gasped as I came, shooting cum over her fingers.

She kneeled and slowly licked my cock. Then she took me in her mouth. Feeling her hands cupping my balls and her lips and tongue caressing my cock, I had to have her. Even though he'd known Lea was my woman, Eddy had pursued her in secret. He hadn't given my feelings the slightest consideration. Why shouldn't I return the favor? I was going to fuck her all damn night until my cock was sore and her pussy lips were red and swollen and my cum seeped out of her cunt.

Sensing my surrender, she drew away from me with a sensuous smile playing about her soft pink lips. I could see the tip of her tongue as she rose. Before the night was over, I'd be thrusting my cock between those pretty lips and hosing down her throat.

But first I would have that bare cunt fuck and fill her with cum. This time, despite her protest, I was going to take her anal virginity.

She walked across the room and leaned over the back of the sofa with her legs parted and her small, cute ass on display. She smiled at me over her shoulder. "Take your clothes off. I want to admire that big, sculptured body of yours with those long legs and that tight ass. Then bring that big monster cock of yours over here and fuck me until I weep."

I briefly considered using the excuse that I needed time to recuperate before I could come again, but when I'm really horny, I don't need much time to recharge my batteries. And I was horny as hell. Besides, God help me, I couldn't resist her.

There was still a small part of my brain that insisted I couldn't go any further, but with my cock hard and hungry, I wasn't listening. It would take an act of God to stop me from fucking her now. I'd deal with the consequences later.

I pushed myself away from the door and quickly undressed. With my cock bouncing in front of my body like a hard nine-inch pole, I hurried across the room to the sofa.

I moved to stand behind her and stroked my fingers between her legs. I fingered her slit. Her cunt was flooded. I withdrew my fingers and bent my legs to get into position to thrust up into her with one hard plunge. I gripped my cock and I slid it along her slit.

She was so hot and horny, pussy juice coated the head of my shaft. She moaned with lust and wiggled her hips. "Oh, yes, baby. Yes. Do it now. Now. Ram that hard pole of yours all the way in me with one plunge. Fuck me hard enough to hurt me. Make me cry with lust and pain. Tear this pussy up and brand it and me as yours."

Her desire for painful sex had always unnerved me a little. While I love hard, no-holds barred sex as well as the next man, I'm not into intentionally inflicting pain on a lover. In addition to enjoying a hard, raunchy fuck sans a condom.

Yes, I know it's crazy. I haven't indulged in unprotected sex in over seven long years, but a man can dream, can't he?

Where was I? Oh, yes, I prefer making slow love to my woman so she enjoys every deep, leisurely thrust. I like to make my woman's toes curl and her back arch as she shatters around me, coming all over me. There are few things sweeter than having your dick buried balls deep in a hot, tight, coming pussy.

But if Lea wanted to be fucked, I'd fuck her until her damned knees knocked. I pressed my cock against her entrance. She slid her hips back slightly. The head of my shaft slipped between the lips of her sex.

Damn, it had been so long since I'd fucked such a sweet cunt. I cupped my hands over her small breasts and slowly slid into her. I closed my eyes, enjoying invading each inch of her tight box.

With her pussy stretched taut over me, I licked the side of her neck. I slid one hand down her body in search of her clit. Rubbing my thumb over it, I drew my hips backward so that only my tip remained inside her.

"Oh, Jake. Jake. Give it to me."

I gave it to her, pushing my entire length back into her.

Fully impaled on me, she wiggled her ass wildly, tightening her vaginal muscles around me. I could feel her pussy juices flowing over my cock.

I gritted my teeth and fought hard not to come. I needed this fuck to last as long as possible.

I jumped guiltily when the phone on the end table beside the sofa rang.

"Ignore it," she ordered, reaching back to stroke my thigh.

I glanced at the caller ID and stiffened. Bree. I was tempted to obey Lea's command, but only for a moment. I'm not sure why or even where I got the strength to stop fucking her. Holding my cock still inside her, I picked up the phone. "Hello?"

"I'm glad I caught you, Jake. I'm running a little late. Can you pick me up half an hour later at six-thirty?"

Perfect. I could finish fucking Lea's sweet cunt before I picked up Bree. "No problem."

"Is something wrong?"

"No. Why do you ask?"

"You sound breathless. Are you sure everything's all right? Do you need to talk?"

Talking was the last thing I wanted.

"Jake? I know something's wrong. Talk to me and tell me what it is. I can't help if you don't. Are you about to do something you shouldn't?"

I wanted to tell her to leave me the fuck alone, but I couldn't. Her soft, caressing voice washed over with me the force of ice-cold water. My head cleared. I looked down at my cock protruding from between the pale cheeks of my only brother's wife and shuddered with revulsion and shame. I'd crossed a line no man should ever cross—regardless of the temptation.

Sucking in a deep, painful breath, I jerked away from Lea and sank down onto the edge of the end table. "No. I'm fine now. I'll see you at six-thirty."

"Jake? Are you sure?"

Damn. It was almost as if she knew I'd been fucking Lea. "I'll be fine. Bye."

I hung up.

"Who the hell was that?"

I turned to find Lea glaring at me. "Bree. We have a date." I glanced at my watch. "In about an hour and a half so let yourself out." I rose and turned away.

"Where the fuck do you think you're going, Jake?" She grabbed my arm. "Don't you dare walk away from me before I've come. You're going to fuck me at least once and if you do a good job, I just might let you out of my pussy in time to arrive fashionably late for your *date* with Bree."

I jerked away and faced her. "Hell will freeze over before I fuck my only brother's wife."

"In case you've forgotten, you were fucking me pretty good before. If you think that frigid bitch is going to let you fuck her tonight, you can think again."

I recalled the feel of Bree's plush, well-padded body against mine. There was no way Lea or anyone else was going to convince me she was frigid. But even if she were, once we were both in bed, I'd warm her up and keep her hot.

"You pushed me too far when I was weak, but it won't happen again."

"The hell it won't. I want some cock, Jake."

"You've had all you're getting. I'm going to shower. If you're not gone when I get back, I will physically pick you up and toss you out on your narrow, flat ass."

Her green eyes narrowed. "You're mine, Jake and I will be damned if I'll let that conniving bitch take you from me."

"You're calling her a bitch again?"

"Yes, I'm calling her a bitch. All the greedy bitch wants is your cock."

"She had a funny way of showing it when she slammed the door in my face last night and even refused to allow me to kiss her."

Her eyes widened. "Kiss her? You tried to kiss her? Why would you want to kiss her?"

"Why do you think?"

She blinked at me. "You really want to fuck her?"

"Isn't that what you had in mind when you set up our blind date?"

"No. She's sneaky. She knew if she gave it up too soon, you'd lose interest. Playing hard to get keeps you interested. I'll be damned if I'll let her anywhere near your cock." She marched across the room and wrapped her fingers around me. "This is mine and I won't have you fucking anyone but me."

I peeled her fingers off my shaft. "Are you losing your mind, Lea? You dumped me for Ed. If I were you I'd worry about who he's fucking."

She gasped. "Are you implying he's cheating on me?"

I doubted he was. He was too much in love with her, but her calling Bree a frigid bitch had pissed me off. I shrugged. "Put your clothes on and see yourself out."

"You're not leaving me like this."

"Watch me." I turned and ignoring my protesting cock, I left the room. In case Lea got any ideas about joining me and testing my new resolve, I pushed the dresser behind my closed bedroom door and went into the bathroom.

As the cold water of the shower cascaded over my head, I blasted myself. Fucking her was the ultimate betrayal. I couldn't think of anything more disgusting than fucking your brother's wife. Granted Lea was a shameless bitch with no morals, but Ed was my flesh and blood. How the hell had I allowed Lea to lead me around by my cock like some horny teenager?

I soaped up my cock and slowly jerked myself off. Then I took a long, warm shower. As I dried off, I thanked God that Bree's call had come in time to keep me from actually coming inside her. As it was, I would have had a difficult time forgiving myself for what I had done.

Bree

Frowning, I put the phone down. I glanced at my bedside clock. It was five o'clock and I was already dressed. Despite my desire not to get involved with Jake, I was eager to see him. So what had made me call and ask him to pick me up half an hour later?

Gabrielle, if you're not careful, you'll lose your head over him. And we can't have that. So get it together, girl. You can have a little fun with him tonight. Maybe share a few kisses and let him cop a feel or two, but that's it. End of story.

Chapter Four

Jake

I arrived for my date with Bree with flowers and a box of chocolates. She gave my arm a squeeze that was almost as potent as if she'd stroked a hand down my thigh near my cock. I was so horny the most innocent touch or glance from her was likely to make me rock hard in seconds if I didn't stop thinking about sex, sex, and even more damned sex.

She accepted the flowers and chocolates with a radiant smile. "Thank you. Have a seat while I put the flowers in water and the chocolates in the refrigerator."

I was too revved up to sit so I paced her living room until she returned. She wore a pink pantsuit that fell around her ample curves in graceful waves. She looked good in pink.

She tilted her head and frowned at me. "What?"

"What?" I shrugged. "What do you mean what?"

"You're staring. Is my nose shiny or something?"

"No."

"Then why are you staring?"

"Why does a man usually stare at a woman?"

She shook her head. "I know it's not because I leave you breathless."

"I'm feeling very breathless at the moment."

She shook her head again. "Don't do that."

"Don't do what?"

"Insincere flattery is—"

"It's not insincere."

"Whatever it is...why are you staring?"

I shrugged. I'd know in the future not to waste time trying to charm a woman who refused to be flattered. "Your call tonight saved me from making what would probably have been the biggest mistake of my life."

She blinked. "Really?"

Actually, it had saved me from compounding the mistake. I nodded.

"What did I stop you from doing?"

I shook my head. "It doesn't matter. I just wanted to thank you."

She sighed. "I don't know why I called."

I arched a brow. "Losing your memory at your age?"

"Cute. Real cute, Jake."

I grinned. "Why, thank you, Bree. I'm glad you think I'm cute."

She rolled her eyes.

I laughed. "Okay. I'm just trying to help jog that memory of yours. You called me because you were running late."

She shook her head again. "Actually, I was already dressed when I called you."

I frowned. "Then why did you call?"

"This is going to sound crazy, but I don't know what made me call you."

I did. Mom often said God looked out for fools and drunks. I had definitely been a fool for succumbing to Lea. I offered her my arm. "Are you ready?"

She nodded. "Where are we going?"

"There's a jazz club on the waterfront."

"Mackies?"

"You've been there?"

"No, but I've always wanted to go."

"Great. That's our destination."

She slipped her arm through mine and smiled up at me. "Maybe the evening won't be a bore after all."

She looked so sexy and provocative I longed to kiss us both breathless. I didn't think she was ready for that so I slapped her ass instead.

"Hey." She danced away from me and rubbed a palm over her cheek. "That stung."

I shrugged and grinned at her. "Let that be a lesson to you."

She tilted her head, her dark eyes locking with mine. "About what?"

"About not flirting with me unless you're prepared to accept the consequences."

I watched her slowly lick her lips. "I wasn't flirting with you."

"The hell you weren't."

"If you're going to get delusional on me..." she allowed her voice to trail off and turned away.

I followed her, caught her arm, and turned her to face me. "What?"

She stared silently up at me, her dark eyes wide, her full lips slightly parted. Damn she looked sweet like that.

I released her arm and palmed the cheek I'd slapped.

She gasped and stepped away from me. "Don't do that."

I drew her against me, slipping both hands over her ass. "Why not? Don't you like being touched?"

"I like it just fine, but—"

"So do I." I rubbed my palms over her ass. Damn. It was big and round. I longed to feel her bare cheeks against my palms and fingers.

She shook her head and pulled out of my arms. "If we're going, we should go."

"What's wrong?"

"I don't know what Lea told you about me, but we're either going out for the evening or you are leaving alone-now. Your choice, Jake."

And this was the woman Lea wanted me to believe was just after my cock? I offered her my arm. "Let's go."

She hesitated. "No hard feelings?"

"It's not my feelings that are hard at the moment, Bree."

"Then what? Oh. You mean your..." She trailed off, her lips twitching.

"I'm glad you find my present state of discomfort amusing."

"Sorry." Her dark eyes danced with amusement as she approached.

I had the last word or should I say slap? As she walked past me towards the door, I slapped both her ass cheeks.

When she gasped and swung around to face me, her dark eyes flashing at me, I reached out and pinched both nipples. They immediately pebbled against my fingers. I smiled down at her, rolling them between my fingers. "Now we're even."

She caught her breath, slapped my hands away and rushed down the hall towards the front door.

I followed slowly, smiling.

When I joined her at the door, she picked up her purse from the table by the door, opened the door and silently stepped into the hallway.

I followed and waited as she locked the door. Then I offered her my arm.

She hesitated. "Can I trust you not to touch my ass again tonight?"

I shrugged. "Sure."

She nodded and slipped her arm through mine.

I smiled. *That's right baby, come to Jake.*

Bree

I loved the atmosphere at Mackies. The food was good and the music wonderful. As he had been the night before, Jake was quiet and barely touched his food. After all the flirting and sexual entrees we'd shared while at my place, I found his silence confusing. I was struggling to make conversation when he abruptly rose and extended his hand. "Dance with me?"

I glanced up, noted the look of desire in his eyes, and caught my breath. Recalling how he'd rubbed my ass earlier and made my nipples hard, I knew what he wanted wasn't a dance. He wanted a slow grind. Since I was feeling a little horny too, I placed my hand in his, and rose. He linked his fingers through mine and held my hand as we walked to the dance floor.

I was twenty-seven and hadn't had my hand held in public since college. I'd forgotten how nice it felt to hold hands with a man.

On the dance floor, I turned towards him, and sighed softly as he slipped his arms around me. He's big and well built. I loved the feel of his body—especially the beginning of the bulge I could feel between his legs. I closed my eyes and pressed my cheek against his shoulder.

He tightened his arms around me, drawing me so close I found myself wondering what his naked body would feel like against mine. I swallowed hard at the thought and moistened my lips. *Okay, girl, keep your grip on reality. I don't care how good his body feels or how horny you are, there's not going to be any sex tonight. So deal with it.*

The lights on the dance floor dimmed and the deejay announced it was the beginning of Mackie's Quiet Storm for lovers. I lifted my head and glanced up to find Jake staring down at me.

I couldn't read the expression in his eyes because of the dimmed lighting, but I could feel the tension in his body. He could probably feel mine as well.

When he slipped both of his palms over my ass and pulled me closer to him, I closed my eyes and pressed my cheek against his shoulder. He moved his palms slowly over my ass. I pressed closer to him and bit my lips to silence a moan of desire.

We danced for what felt like hours. The longer we danced, the more aroused I became. At one point, I realized I could feel the outline of his cock. Lord, he felt long and thick. And I wanted to feel it against me-in me-deep in my pussy. I bit my lip, lost my head, and ground my pussy against him.

I realized what I was doing and froze, my cheeks burning. I pushed against his shoulders.

Although he allowed me to draw away from his cock, he kept his palms on my ass. "What's wrong?"

He could ask that when he had an ass cheek in each hand and I'd just ground myself against him like a hussy in heat?

"Nothing, but it must be getting late."

"So? Why is that a problem? Do you have a boyfriend waiting for you at home?"

The question annoyed me. "I don't cheat. If I had a boyfriend, I wouldn't be here with you. "

He slapped my ass.

I sucked in a breath and glared up at him. "You promised not to do that again tonight."

He released my left ass cheek to rub his thumb against my bottom lip. "I lied. So what's the problem?"

"Who says there is one? Because I want to leave there must be a problem?"

He started to shake his head, then shrugged instead. "You want to leave? Fine." He released me.

His voice sounded terse and annoyed. So I was surprised, but pleased when he linked his fingers through mine as we walked back to our table.

After all those slow, intimate dances, his holding my hand felt highly sensual. At our table, I reluctantly peeled my fingers from his. "I need to freshen up."

He nodded.

Noting the gleam in his eyes, I was hesitant to turn my back on him. I leaned close and hissed at him. "You'd better keep your hands off my ass."

He arched a brow. "Or?"

"If you slap my ass now—"

"You'll have a slapped ass."

I sucked in a breath, feeling my cheeks heat up. "Jake—"

He lifted his hands and held them palm out. "I won't slap your ass the moment you turn your back. Satisfied?"

Strangely enough, I wasn't.

"Don't you believe me?"

I did. So I nodded and turned slowly away, and was disappointed when he didn't slap my ass as I walked away.

After I visited the ladies room while he took care of the bill, we left. Just outside the club, he reached for my hand.

I stared straight ahead, smiling. I could easily get used to having him hold my hand and slapping my ass. When he held the passenger door of his car open for me, he stood so close I had to brush against him to get into the car. The temptation to turn to him and rub against his hard-on was difficult to resist. But I did and slipped into the car.

After he closed the passenger door, I watched him walk around the hood of the car, turning to glance at him when he slid into the driver's seat. He turned to look at me. I met his intense stare briefly before I looked away and reached for my seatbelt.

I was so unnerved I couldn't get the seatbelt fastened.

"Let me help you."

I shook my head. "No. It's okay. I've almost got it."

As I continued to struggle to fasten it, he reached over and secured the seatbelt. Instead of moving back to his seat, he bent his head and brushed his lips against the corner of my mouth.

Surrendering to a shock of desire, I tilted my head, and leaned into him.

His warm, insistent lips moved over mine with a slow hunger that made rational thought difficult. Pressing me back against the seat, he leaned forward and deepened the kiss. He kissed me again and again, each kiss more demanding.

Just as I felt the tip of his tongue touch mine, his big hands moved between our bodies to cup my breasts. His palms seemed to burn my skin — even through my silk top and bra. I moaned and stroked my hands over his chest, feeling my nipples tighten.

Still kissing me, his fingers probed the buttons of my blouse.

While I tried to convince myself that it was time to stop him, I felt his hands inside my blouse. He brushed his fingers against my cleavage before he deftly popped my breasts out of my bra, and cupped them in his hands.

He lifted them and bent his head.

I moaned, consumed with desire as he probed my left nipple with the tip of his tongue. I cupped my hands over the back of his head, stroking my fingers through his dark hair. It was soft and silky. I curled my fingers in it. I shuddered, my pussy flooding as his warm lips settled over my left nipple.

He sucked gently, allowing his tongue to sweep along my breast in slow, sweet circles. Waves of pleasure crashed over me. When he stroked a hand down my body, I willingly parted my legs. He released my seatbelt and eased the fingers of one hand into my pants and under my panties.

Moving his mouth to my other breast, he flicked his thumb against my clit.

"Hmmm."

After kissing my breast, he sucked my nipple between his lips.

I closed my eyes on a rush of delight as his probing fingers found my slit, and eased into my pussy. "Oooh."

He tore his lips away from my breast. When I opened my eyes and blinked at him, he bent his head and closed his lips over mine. As he burned kiss after kiss against my mouth, he gently finger fucked me. Overcome with lust, I moaned, and reached between our bodies to cup a trembling hand between his thighs.

I could feel his cock stretched along one leg through his pants. Awed by his size and girth, I had to touch him. I struggled to slide down his zipper and eagerly reach into his pants. I greedily pushed my hands into the waistband of his briefs. I gasped as my fingers encountered his cock. Lord, he was long, thick, and so rigid, I was hard pressed not to rip off my clothes, part my legs, and moan with mindless lust as he thrust his naked cock deep into my aching cunt.

I'm not sure how far I would have gone if the sounds of laughter coming from several patrons leaving the club hadn't shocked me back to my senses. I gasped, pulled my hands from his pants, and jerked back against my seat.

He swore softly and lifted his head. Giving me an intense stare that I couldn't maintain, he zipped up his pants and moved into his seat.

I pushed my breasts back into my bra and fastened my blouse. I had to take several deep breaths to calm my racing heart before I managed to fasten my seatbelt.

He sat with his seatbelt on and his hands clenched on the steering wheel for several moments before he started the car and drove out of the parking lot.

After what we'd just shared, I found his silence unsettling. Why didn't he say something? Anything? I was fairly certain I knew what he was feeling, but what was he thinking? Had our sweet interlude changed his opinion of me?

I turned to stare at his profile. His lack of emotion made it difficult to feel anything but regret for what I'd just allowed to happen. I closed my eyes and bit my lip. I'm not a prude, but to come so close to having sex in a car on a second date at my age was my standard definition of sleazy, alley cat behavior. He had to think I was easy. I compressed my lips. Well, I wasn't.

Jake

Ignoring the urge to take my right hand off the steering wheel and slip it between Bree's legs, I kept my gaze on the road. But I was very aware of her. I swallowed slowly, hard pressed not to stop the car on some dark street, pull her into the back seat, and thrust my naked cock deep into her pussy. I was so eager to fuck her, I could almost taste my hunger for her pussy. My only consolation on the drive to her apartment was the knowledge that I'd soon be buried balls deep in her pussy. Granted, I hadn't a hope in hell of fucking her without a condom–at least not this early in our relationship.

At the time I was so damned horny, the impact of that thought didn't hit me until much later. The thirty-minute drive to her apartment seemed to last forever. When I parked behind her complex, I sighed. Relief was only moments away.

I guessed I should have known I might be in for a nasty let down when she shook her head as I reached for her hand when I opened the passenger side door for her. But I'm not the brightest guy on the block when I have blue balls. And at the moment, my balls were as blue as they'd ever been.

So, although I was surprised at her refusal to let me hold her hand, I wasn't overly concerned. She might be one of those women who didn't want her neighbors knowing who she was sleeping with. As she walked a little to my left and in front of me, I was hard pressed not to reach out and slap that big ass of hers.

Chapter Five

Jake

Reality and rage settled on me like a second skin at her apartment door. She flashed a brief, insincere smile at me and offered me her hand. "Thanks for a...nice evening."

I took her hand in mine and drew her towards me. I was almost as eager to taste her luscious lips again as I was to fuck her.

She jerked her hand from mine and stepped back. "Good...night."

I stared at her, feeling a wall of rage slowly consuming me. "Good night? Why the hell are you telling me good night? What the hell am I missing? Thirty minutes earlier, you were all over me. Now you expect me to go home and take a damned cold shower? Are you out of your mind?"

She sighed. "I know I might have led you on a little, but—"

"You might have led me on a little? Woman, what is your problem? You had your hands wrapped around my cock like—"

She lifted her chin. "I know where my hand was and I admit I probably led you on, but it was a mistake. I'm sorry."

"You're sorry? What the hell good does that do me? Why the hell did you lead me on if you planned to slam the door in my face again? Do you get off on pulling this shit on your dates? I guess we know why you don't have a man in your life, don't we?"

She gasped and lifted her right hand. For a moment, I half expected her to slap me. At the last minute, she curled her hand into a fist, and stared up at me with a hurt look in her eyes. "You...bastard. You have the nerve to say that just because I won't jump into bed with you on a second damned date?"

What the hell did she have to be hurt about? She led me on again–this time in an ugly way and then expected me not to be angry? She was definitely in league with Lea.

"If I'm a bastard, I guess we both know what that makes you. Don't we? You're clearly a first-class..." Looking down into her wide gaze, as angry as I was and as much as I wanted to shout it, I choked on the word bitch. I couldn't say it, but she must have known what I meant. I glared at her, turned, and stalked away.

I sat in my car in the parking lot, taking long, deep breaths but it didn't help. I was horny and angrier than I could ever remember being. I raked both hands through my hair and closed my eyes. What the hell had I gotten myself into? When I'd first seen her the previous night, I'd wanted to run away from her. Now I wanted to be in her bed so badly I couldn't imagine any other woman being able to blunt some of my sexual frustration.

I briefly considered going to a bar or club to pick up a woman for the night, but I knew in the morning I was still going to be horny and angry because Bree and Lea were jerking me around and I couldn't have either one of them.

Bree had blown me off again and Lea...Lea. Lea was home alone and probably as horny as I was. I sat up and opened my eyes. I knew it was wrong, but what would happen if I surrendered to my lust for her just once more? I'd use a condom and never go near her again. But just this once, I needed to sleep with one of the two women consuming me.

I couldn't have Bree, but damned if I wouldn't have Lea. Just this once. I closed my eyes, offered a silent plea for the sin I was about to commit, and started the car.

Twenty minutes later, I sat outside Ed and Lea's ranch house, trying to talk myself into either going home or going to a bar to pick up a woman. But the woman I wanted wasn't at a bar. She was home with her door closed firmly in my face. I couldn't have Bree and I usually didn't settle for second best, but I was desperate. Had I been thinking rationally then, I would have known I was in big trouble. But I wasn't thinking–at least not with my head.

I got out of my car and walked up the driveway to the front door. As I was about to ring the bell, my cell phone rang.

I wanted to ignore it, but recalling how a well-timed call from Bree had stopped me earlier, I pulled the phone from the clip at my waist. I glanced at the screen and moistened my lips. Bree. Why the hell was she calling me this time? I glanced at the house, hesitated a moment, then walked back down the driveway as I put the phone to my ear.

"What?"

I heard a soft sigh. "You were right and I'm sorry."

I leaned against my car, staring at the back of the house where I could see the light on in what I knew was Ed and Lea's bedroom. Ed and Lea's bedroom.

"Why are you calling me? Haven't you had enough fun at my expense?"

"If you think sending you away was easy for me, you're wrong. But I don't sleep around and I don't sleep with strangers."

"Then why the hell are you calling me? What makes you think I'm interested in hearing you say you're sorry after you spent the entire evening leading me on and flirting with me?"

"Because I am."

"That's doesn't do me or my blue balls a lot of good...unless you've changed your mind. Have you? Do you want me to come back?"

"No. I haven't changed my mind."

"Then we have nothing else to say to each other." I ended the call and turned off my phone. I sighed. As annoying as I found Bree's call, it had given me time to get my lust under control. If nothing else, I could thank her for keeping me from sleeping with Lea again. The damned harpy seemed to have a knack for ensuring I kept the blue balls she gave me.

I got back in my car and quickly drove home before I could change my mind. At home, I undressed, masturbated, took a cool shower, and fell into bed. I tried to keep my thoughts clear, but my last waking thoughts were of Bree. Damn. I slept through what was left of the night and woke the next day longing to see her.

I spent the morning fighting the desire. I went to the gym and worked out, spent time in the sauna, and returned home just after twelve. I still wanted to see her. Although I knew I hadn't a hope in hell of that happening, I called her anyway.

Bree

After a long, restless night, most of which I spent wishing I hadn't let Jake leave, I was in a foul mood. I had no idea what was happening between us. I knew why I'd refused to sleep with him, but I had no idea what had made me call him after he'd stormed away from me. Earlier he'd said I'd saved him from making a huge mistake. Had my second call stopped him from making another one? If so, what had he been about to do?

Why should you care? There's no way he'll come anywhere near you after that stunt you pulled last night. You're lucky he didn't do worse than almost call you a bitch. Another man might have actually called you a bitch—while he was raping you.

I sat at my vanity table, staring at my reflection. Recalling the intensity of his kisses, I closed my eyes. *Oh, lord, girl, you are so stupid. A handsome hunk was eager to fuck you and you get on your high horse and ramble on and on about how you don't sleep around. Fine. You don't sleep around. What good did that do you last night? And it's not helping that much right now either.*

I jumped as the phone rang. Shaking my head, I got up and picked the cordless phone up from my nightstand. "Hello?"

"Hi."

I sucked in a quick breath as I recognized Jake's voice. "Hi."

"Ah, I guess it's my turn to apologize for my behavior last night and to ask you—"

"No. Considering...you behaved better than I deserved. I really didn't set out to...tease you."

"What did you set out to do?"

I decided admitting I'd just wanted to fool around a little might not be a good idea. "I just wanted to get to know you. I know I...left you in a bad way, but if it's any consolation, I had a miserable night too."

He sighed. "So we're both sorry."

"Yes."

"I'm in the mood to take a drive and maybe have lunch in Penny Pack Park. Are you feeling like a drive and a picnic?"

We should probably have a cooling off period before we saw each other again. But if I refused his invitation, it might be the last one I received. After the miserable night I'd spent filled with regrets, I knew I didn't want that. "Yes."

He sighed. "Great. Can I pick you up in half an hour?"

"Make it an hour."

"I'll see you then. I need to thank you again. After I left you I was in pretty bad shape and if you hadn't called me again..."

"What were you going to do and how many times do you expect me to pull your bacon out of the pan?"

He laughed. "I'll see you soon."

"So you're not going to tell me?"

"No. I'm not."

"Why not?"

"It's not something a man admits to a woman he's trying to impress."

"Since when have you wanted to impress me?"

"Since the moment you slammed the door in my face."

"I didn't slam the door in your face."

"Yes. You did."

I shook my head. "We can argue about that later. So you're not going to tell me what I saved you from? Is it that bad?"

"I'm sure you'd...yes, it is and I don't want you to refuse to see me again if I tell you."

I probably should have run like hell in the opposite direction then and there.

"I'll pick you up in an hour."

"Actually, you'd better make it two hours so I have time to make sandwiches."

"You bring blankets. I'll take care of lunch and I'll see you in an hour."

Was he eager to see me? I smiled. "Okay."

Jake

You have got to be the biggest idiot in the entire state of Pennsylvania. She jerks you around two nights in a row. And what do you do? Go back for more. What the hell is wrong with you? She's not even pretty and she could stand to lose some weight. So why are you panting over her like a damned dog in heat?

I frowned, shrugged, and got out of my car at Bree's complex. I had no idea what kept pulling me back to her. I just knew I was excited and aroused at the thought of seeing her again...kissing her again...holding her...fucking her all night long. Of course, the way my luck had been going during that weekend, she'd probably lead me on and then send me home with another set of blue balls.

If you think that, what the hell are you doing here? Even as I asked myself the question, I kept walking towards her building. Ten minutes later, she opened her apartment door and gave me a radiant smile that sent my lust off the scale.

"Hi, Jake."

She wore a green, loose-fitting pants suit. Damn, she looks good in green. Real good.

"Jake? Are those for me?"

I blinked and smiled. "Sorry. Hi. Yes." I gave her the bouquet of flowers.

She tilted her head. "Do you always shower a woman with so many flowers in one weekend?"

"No."

She arched a brow. She has nice brows. They're arched, but otherwise natural. "Why not?"

"I can't remember ever seeing one woman three days in a row."

"Oh. Well, I admit you're the first man who's asked me out on three consecutive days." She put a hand on my arm and leaned close. "Tell me. What makes me special?"

Just what the hell was it about this woman that aroused me so quickly? I shrugged and slapped her left ass cheek. "I have no idea."

She gasped and squeezed my arm. "Maybe we'll find out together." She stepped back and half turned away from me. She glanced at me over her shoulder and wiggled her hips. "You forgot one."

I knew I was letting myself in for a big fall, but I couldn't seem to stop myself. I lifted my hand and slapped her neglected ass cheek. "Satisfied?"

She licked her lips and averted her gaze. "I'll put these in water."

I remained by the front door, staring after her. My gaze drifted downward and locked on her ass. Although I'd always preferred slender women with tight, cute asses, my cock stirred as I imagined what her bare bottom would look like.

She abruptly glanced over her shoulder and caught me staring at her rear. She turned to face me.

I lifted my gaze to hers and watched her moisten the full, warm lips I longed to kiss.

"I'll be right back."

I nodded and allowed my gaze to drift down to her breasts. She has the largest breasts I've ever actually seen in person. They're huge. A man could get lost in her cleavage and never want to be found.

"Are you planning to stare at me all day?"

I shrugged. "I can stare or I can touch...caress...and fondle, slap, suck, and fuck. Your choice."

She caught her breath and left the room.

When she returned, she looked everywhere but directly at me and she made a point not to turn her back to me. I wasn't worried. When I felt like slapping that big, round ass of hers again, I would.

"I'm ready," she announced.

I opened the apartment door and stepped aside. "After you."

She slipped passed me sideways.

I laughed and followed her out into the hall.

Two hours later, we were in the park sitting on blankets with our backs against a large tree trunk. She nibbled at one of the chicken salad sandwiches I'd picked up at a deli. I'd eaten half a roast beef sandwich before admitting to myself that my current hunger wasn't for food.

She finished her sandwich, wiped her mouth, and turned to look at me. "Aren't you hungry?"

"Not for food."

She glanced briefly away before turning back to meet my gaze. "What's going on between us?"

I shook my head. "I have no idea."

"Is your interest going to last past the weekend?"

"I don't know," I admitted.

"Is it going to last past your getting what you want?"

"Am I getting what I want today?"

She lowered her lids. "You haven't answered my question."

"Fine. I don't know."

A small smile played over her sweet lips. "Hmmm." She looked up at me, her dark eyes alight with amusement. "You don't know much, do you?"

I half turned and cupped a hand against her cheek. "I know I'm burning for you." I longed to lean forward and kiss her, but decided to allow her to make the first move this time. Maybe that would help ensure I got past first base this time.

She moistened her lips. "We've only known each other three days."

"I've been burning for you for two of those days." I stroked a finger down her face. She has lovely skin. It's dark, smooth, and soft. "Are you going to bust my balls again?"

She cast her gaze downward. When she remained silent, I lifted her chin. "Are you?"

She looked into my eyes. I saw desire in her dark gaze, but she seemed hesitant. Well, I'd help her make up her mind. I bent my head. I'd intended to gently touch my lips to hers. But the moment I felt her soft, warm lips under mine, I lost it. I slipped my arms around her and pressed a hungry kiss against her mouth. When she parted those full, sweet lips, I devoured them.

After several moments of holding her hands curled into fists against my chest, she opened them and slipped her arms around my neck. Her fingers stroking through my hair made me hotter. I eased her onto her back. When she parted her legs and bent her knees, I stretched out on top of her with my aching cock pressed between her thighs.

Grinding my hips against her, I nibbled at her lips.

She moaned softly and humped at me.

She's so sweet and irresistible. I kissed her repeatedly, sucking her tongue into my mouth. That got me so aroused I had to have her. I pushed up her top and worked her breasts from her bra. Damn, they were big and heavy. They sagged, but I didn't care. I just wanted to taste them.

I closed my eyes and buried my face between her cleavage. I licked the insides of her breasts, loving the way they felt against my face. Everything about her from the feel and smell of her skin to the humping of her crotch against me heightened my need for her. I lifted my hips and fumbled between our bodies until I managed to unzip my pants and free my cock. I opened her pants and eased them down before I settled back between her thighs.

She gasped and pushed at my shoulders. "Jake...wait..."

"No more waiting," I groaned. "I'm burning for you."

"No, Jake. No...not here...let me up."

She'd teased me for the last time. There was no way in hell I was allowing her up before I came. But I didn't want to frighten her so I tried to slow down. "It's all right. I'll be gentle," I told her.

"Please, Jake. Not here. We can't do it here."

The hell we couldn't. I was way past the point of no return. "Shhh." I pressed my erect cock against her panties.

She pushed against my shoulders again. "Jake."

Chapter Six

Jake

"It's all right," I said again. "You can keep your panties on and up. I won't penetrate you." But damn if I was going to stop.

She held her body stiff under me. Although she didn't ask me to stop again and she made no further effort to push me off her, I didn't want her regretting our first time together. I cupped my palm under one breast and drew the nipple of the other between my lips. I rubbed my cock against her thigh and sucked her breast, flicking my tongue against her nipple.

"Oooh." She wiggled her hips against mine and slipped her arms around me, holding me close. "Ooooh."

Her soft cries as I humped at her panty-clad pussy made not plunging into the wet pussy so close to my cock that much harder. But I'd given her my word I wouldn't penetrate her. Besides, I was so horny, that when she moaned again and closed her thighs over my cock, I knew I was within seconds of losing it.

She was aroused, but I knew she was nowhere near ready to come. I tried to hold back, but I couldn't. Despite my efforts, I came, spewing load after load of cum all over her panties and thighs. Then I collapsed on top of her, pressing my cheek against hers and slipping my arms around her.

It only took a few moments before the insanity of my climax vanished and I could think of something besides pussy. "Damn. I'm sorry. I don't usually come and leave my partner—"

She pushed against my shoulders. "It's all right, but I'm a bit of a mess...I feel like I have cum all over me. We should get up and leave."

For the first time in my life, I was lying on a full-figured woman instead of a tiny one I had to keep most of my weight off of. I liked feeling her full, sizable curves under me, but I sighed and rolled off her. I lay on my back staring up at the sky while she fumbled with her clothes.

I turned my head. She had her back to me. Did she regret what had just happened? Of course she did. Why wouldn't she when she hadn't gotten a damn thing out of it? I closed my eyes. *Way to go, Jake. Coming before your lover the first time you make love is an ideal way to ensure there won't be a second time.* Damn I wanted—no I needed there to be a second time. There had to be. I had to have intercourse with her at least once. So I needed to make amends and—

"Jake? I need to clean up. We should go."

I pushed my cock into my briefs, zipped up my pants, and sat up.

She was standing with her arms crossed over her breasts, deliberating avoiding my gaze. I think that's when I knew I'd blown whatever chance I might have had with her by my lack of control.

I looked up at her, resting a hand on her thigh. "I know you didn't come, but if you give me a chance, I'll make it up to you. I suck a—"

"No." She shook her head. "It's all right."

The more she said it was all right, the deeper shit I knew I was in. I could see she was in no mood to spend any more time with me. It was time to leave and regroup later. So we gathered up the blankets and the remnants of our picnic, and I carried them back to the car.

As much as I wanted to talk to her on the drive to her apartment, I felt awkward. I hadn't experienced such an embarrassing lack of control in years. I didn't know what to say. So I probably did the worst thing I could. I said nothing. Worse yet, she was silent as well. Whenever I glanced at her, she stared straight ahead. And she still had her arms crossed over her breasts, as if she were protecting them from me.

I had the feeling she'd withdrawn from me mentally and well as physically. Oh, God, I hoped she didn't feel as if I'd forced her. I wanted to ask her, but I was afraid of her answer. After all, she had asked me to stop. And I had refused.

Oh, hell could this weekend get any worse? I knew better than to try to hold her hand as I walked her into her building. At her door, I struggled for words. I knew if I said the wrong thing, she'd never see me again. But I had no idea what was the right thing to say. I only knew I wanted to see her again.

While I struggled to find words that felt right, she pointed to the door behind her. "I'm a real mess...so I'm going to go in now."

I looked at her and sighed when she averted her gaze. Oh, yeah. I'd blown it. "Okay. I...ah...I'll call you tomorrow."

She shook her head. "I'd rather you didn't."

Damn it. "Why not?"

"I don't know why not. I'd just rather you didn't."

"Is it because I didn't stop when you asked me to?"

She jerked her head up, her gaze wide. "If you're asking if I feel like you forced me, no."

Oh, God, what a relief. "Then why can't I call you?"

"Because I asked you to stop and you didn't."

I stared at her. "What? You just said—"

"I said I didn't feel as if you'd raped me. That doesn't mean I appreciate you not stopping when I asked you to."

I shook my head. "What the hell do you want from me?"

"Who says I want anything from you?"

Oh, this shit was getter better all the time. "Bree—"

"No. Look. We spent most of the weekend together. You showered me with flowers, you got your rocks off, and now it's time to move on."

Of course she had to put everything in the worse possible light. I should have just turned and walked away then, but I didn't. I stood there like an idiot trying to make her change her mind. "So you're saying you don't want to see me again?"

She was determined to jerk me around to the very end. Why else would she avoid a direct answer? "I'm saying I'd rather you didn't call me."

"And what if I call you anyway?"

"What if you do as I ask and not call?"

I touched her cheek. "What if I give you a few days and then call?"

"I'm going inside now. Goodbye."

I cupped her cheek and brushed my lips against hers. "I'm sorry. I usually have better control than I displayed this afternoon, but—"

She stepped away from me. "You don't need to keep apologizing. I probably owed you one for last night."

"Well, damn, you certainly have a way with words."

She shrugged. "Whatever. You've had your one and the weekend is over."

Shit. This was sounding too final for me. "Bree—"

"Goodbye, Jake."

Damn if she didn't go inside and close the door in my face again. Damn her. I spun around and walked away. The little bitch had jerked me around for the last damned time. I was going to go to an upscale bar, pick up the prettiest available woman, and fuck her until Bree was just a distant, unpleasant memory.

Bree

After I stood at my bedroom window watching Jake drive out of the parking lot, I undressed. I had cum all over my panties and the tops of my thighs. I'd never had a lover who produced so much seed. As annoyed as I was with his having sexed himself up using me as his toy in broad day-light, I wondered if he always came so copiously. What would he have felt like inside me with his big, hot cock putting out the fire in my pussy with his cum?

That's something you are never going to find out, girl. You had a wild, weekend fling with a handsome, sexy hunk. You didn't come, but he sure as hell gave you a weekend you won't soon forget. But now it's time to get back to reality.

I took my favorite sex toy, a big, waterproof, ebony vibrator, into the shower with me. With the warm water cascading over me, I ran it along my clit, slit, and inner thighs before I slipped it in and out of my pussy. I closed my eyes, imagined the vibrator was a hard, warm cock that belonged to a handsome hunk...Jake...until I came.

While my physical hunger for a climax had been satisfied, I was left with another desire. Sex toys were fine, but they would never take the place of a real lover with warm, insistent lips, a big, masculine body, and a pair of arms holding me tight. They wouldn't quench my desire for sex with someone like...Jake. Damn him.

So why didn't you exercise a little understanding with him? He's not the first man to lose control and come before pleasing you. He probably won't be the last. And you could have taken his inability to control himself with you as a compliment. He wanted to see you again and you kicked him to the curb. It's done. So do not think I'm going to put up with your hanging around here whining about being manless when it's your own fault.

I decided to forget my bittersweet weekend with Jake. I dressed and headed out to the mall. If shopping didn't cheer me up, nothing would.

After spending way too much on clothes I didn't need, I returned home to find Jake had sent me a dozen roses. The card read,

Forgive me? Jake.

There wasn't really anything much to forgive. I think my problem with Jake was I knew he had the potential to really hurt me. I could easily fall hard for him, but when the novelty of his dating and sleeping with a full-figured black woman wore off, and he walked away, I'd be left with a bruised and battered heart.

Surprisingly, I slept well that night. Granted, I thought about Jake as I fell asleep, but I didn't linger awake for hours reliving every second of every kiss we'd shared.

In the morning, I felt ahead of the game because I hadn't wallowed in despair the night before. I had a bowl of oatmeal and a banana before I drove to work feeling upbeat. If I'd managed to keep a hunk like Jake interested all weekend and if I'd gotten him so aroused he couldn't control himself, why shouldn't I be able to attract some Morris Chestnut look-a-like? Thinking of one of the teddies I'd bought, I smiled.

It was a two-piece white lace teddy. The top did a poor job of providing support, but it did a fair one of showcasing my large, heavy breasts. The bottom was like a one-legged leotard. The left leg ended just above my ankle. The right side was legless and fit that side like a panty-with a hole in the crotch.

Hopefully I'd find someone I could wear it for soon. I quickly dismissed thoughts of Jake. That bit of weekend madness was over. It had probably been a mistake to ask him not to call me, but I wasn't going to beat myself up over it.

My mood darkened when I arrived at work and found Lea waiting for me. I don't know how I knew or even why I thought I knew it, but watching her, I had a sudden, horrifying feeling that she was somehow involved with Jake's near sins. I didn't like to think he was the kind of man who would have an affair with his brother's wife, but if ever a woman could tempt a man into sin, it was Lea. Didn't big men like Jake always like tiny women like her? I could imagine her easily wrapping Jake around and around her little finger until he was hers to do with as she liked.

"Lea." My voice sounded cold and unwelcoming. I stopped and started again. "Lea, this is a surprise."

She rose and stared me at up and down. "Is it? Is it really?"

"Yes. It is. What can I do for you so early in the morning? Need help with a project?"

"I'm perfectly capable of taking care of my own work."

Fine. Then what the hell did she and her attitude want? I forced myself to smile and tried to look pleasant. "Of course you are."

She shook her head angrily. "Jake won't talk to me."

"No?"

"No and I know it has something to do with you."

Now she was starting to get on my nerves. "Why would his not talking to you have anything to do with me?"

Her eyes flashed angrily. "I know it has something to do with you and I want to know what happened between you two this weekend."

I put my briefcase and shoulder bag down on the desk and faced her. "Funny, I was going to ask you the same thing."

"What? What do you mean? What are you...suggesting?"

Just the way she answered that question and glanced around with a guilty look on her face crystallized my certainty there was something between her and Jake. "You're not sleeping with your own brother-in-law. Are you?"

She gasped, glared at me, and rushed away.

I sank down at my desk, feeling my shoulders slump. *Oh, Jake, how could you? How could you with your brother's wife?* It's true he'd said I'd saved him from a bad sin, but what kind of man had to be saved from sleeping with his own brother's wife? Clearly, Jake was a very flawed individual. He was also a very attractive, hard-to-forget one.

The week went downhill from there. It was difficult to concentrate on work. Often, when I needed a clear head the most, I found myself thinking of Jake. I hated that I was still attracted to him knowing what he was capable of. After all, how did I know he hadn't actually slept with Lea? She'd been very territorial when she'd confronted me.

Each time Lea and I met during the week, she gave me the deep freeze treatment like I'd injured her in some way. She was sleeping with her husband's brother and I was the bad guy? She and Jake were both flawed and immoral. They probably deserved each other. I felt sorry for the brother.

By the time Friday rolled around, I felt tired and beat down. I just wanted to spend the weekend pampering myself by sleeping late, eating whatever I wanted, taking long soaks in the tub, and losing myself in a good erotic romance where the hero was a skillful lover who did not come before the heroine and was not swayed by outward appearances only—as that damned Jake so clearly was.

As I kicked off my heels in my bedroom on Friday evening, my phone rang. I groaned. I was not in the mood to talk. I considered letting my answering machine pick up, but decided it might be my mother. I sank down on the side of the bed and caught my breath as I glanced at the caller ID.

I didn't recognize the number, but I recognized the area code. I took a deep breath and picked up the phone. "Hello?"

"Gabrielle. Hi."

Despite my confusion and bad mood, I smiled at the sound of Darren's warm, deep baritone. "Darren. Hello. How are you? It's so good to hear from you."

"I was hoping you'd feel that way."

"Of course I do." I sat on the bed with my back against the headboard. "How are you?"

"Okay. How are you?"

It wouldn't do to admit I was lousy. "I'm...good. How's California treating you?"

"It's a beautiful place, but I miss Philly. That's home."

I nodded. I'd spent four years at a university in Alabama. That too was a beautiful state, but I'd always known when I graduated I was coming home to the City of Brotherly Love. "I know what you mean. So, how's work?"

"I have a handle on things now. A good one so I've earned some vacation time. I thought I might spend some of it at home."

"Oh."

"I'm sure you're dating now, but is it serious?"

"Darren..."

"I only asked because I'd really like to see you while I'm in town. If you're dating but it's not serious, I thought...I hoped..."

Was I dating anyone? Was it serious? I knew I'd seen the last of Jake and if it I hadn't, I had no illusions about whatever we'd shared turning into anything more than a casual fling—at least from his point of view. Besides, if he were sleeping with Lea, I sure as hell didn't want anything to do with him.

I chose my words carefully. "I'm not involved in a serious relationship with anyone, Darren, but I'm still not interested in a long distance relationship."

I stopped and bit my lip. Where the hell had that come from? Hadn't I all but decided to see Darren again if he called? Why was I allowing that disastrous last "date" with Jake to change my mind? Lea hadn't been at work that day. I knew because I'd had to finish a project of hers. She'd probably spent the day wrapped in Jake's arms. Even as I tried to harden myself to him, a part of me cried out that he wouldn't. He couldn't. Surely he was far better than that even if she weren't.

"I see."

I thought of Jake with Lea and spoke in a rush. "But that might not mean we can't...share intimacy for old time's sake...with protection."

"I understand."

I closed my eyes briefly, wondering if I'd done the right thing. "When are you coming?"

"If all goes well here, in about six weeks. I know a lot can change in that time, so I'll call before I come to make sure it's still all right to come."

"I look forward to seeing you again, Darren."

We said goodbye and hung up. There. It was done. When Darren came home I'd sleep with him. To hell with Jake Volmer.

I dragged my thoughts from Jake, turning them back to Darren. He was tall, dark, and attractive. Besides, he was a good and considerate lover. Thank God he was still interested in me.

Recalling our last time making love, I smiled and closed my eyes. It would be nice to see him again and feel his big, dark body on top of mine...feel his warm lips...his thick, hard cock sliding into my...

Bbrrring.

Startled, I opened my eyes and sat up. I glanced at the caller ID. Jake. I bit my lip. What did he want? Did I want to talk to him? I decided to let the answering machine pick up. I left the bedroom, closing the door behind me before I heard his voice and weakened.

I made myself a drink in the living room and sank down into the recliner. I turned off the lights and turned on the TV. The phone rang again. I glanced at the caller ID. It was Jake again. I took a deep breath, moistened my lips, and finally picked it up. "Hello."

Chapter Seven

Jake

"Hi, Bree. This is Jake."

"I thought we agreed not to see each other again. I—"

"I never agreed to that. I told you I'd give you a few days and then call you."

I sighed. Why didn't I just tell him I wasn't interested and hang up?

"Are you busy tonight?"

"I...well, actually, I..."

"If not, I was hoping you'd have dinner with me."

"That probably would not be a good idea."

"Why not?"

Why not indeed? Maybe because he'd spent the day in Lea's bed? "Did you work today?"

"Yes."

"All day?"

"Yes. Why do you ask? Did you try to call me?"

I decided to be honest with him. "No, but I have a feeling you're having an affair."

"You think I'm having an affair? With who?"

"With Lea." I spat the words out, making no effort to keep the disgust out of my voice.

He swore softly. "Is that what she told you?"

So did that mean it was true? He was actually sleeping with his own brother's wife? "So, it's true." I closed my eyes and swallowed hard. "Isn't it?"

He went on in a cold, hard voice. "Hell no, it's not true. She'd like you to believe it is, but it's not."

"Why? Why would she want me or anyone else to believe something so awful if it wasn't true?"

"Because she's a soulless bitch determined to make me miserable."

"And?"

He sighed. "And it was almost true."

"Oh, Jake. How could you?"

"I said almost. Almost, but it never happened. I'm not having an affair with her or anyone else."

"But?"

"I don't want to talk about this."

"And I do."

He sighed again. "Fine. I'm not having an affair with her, but we were involved before she married my brother."

"Involved how?"

"Bree—"

"We can talk about it now or you can hang up and don't bother calling me again." There. Now he knew where I stood with this damned Lea shit.

"Bree—"

"Involved how?"

He swore angrily.

"I'm still waiting for you to make your choice, Jake."

"We were lovers. Is that what you wanted to hear? Are you satisfied now?"

"No." The thought of the two of them together made me...I felt a jealous, angry knot tightening in my belly. "Is that the mistake you almost made twice? Sleeping with your brother's wife?"

"Look, Bree—"

"Is it?"

"If I say yes?"

"Is it?"

"You're determined to have everything your own damned way, aren't you?"

"Yes. Yes, I am. Now answer the damned question, Jake or fuck the hell off." I felt like I was demanding answers to questions I had no right to ask, but I was angry and jealous and I wanted him to know up front I wasn't taking any shit from him.

There was an extended silence before he spoke. "Yes. Now are you satisfied?"

His voice sounded cold and angry. Tough shit. He wasn't going to play me. "That depends."

"It depends? On what? What the fuck do you want from me?"

"The truth. If you can handle it."

"Look, you—"

"Don't you call me *you* in that tone. If you don't like the way the conversation is going, you can always hang up."

There was another silence, during which I kept expecting to hear him slam his receiver down. Instead, he swore again. "Fine. What does it depend on?"

He didn't sound like a happy camper, but he hadn't hung up. I felt part of the knot loosening. I softened my voice. "Can you promise me that you've never slept with your brother's wife?"

"Yes. Yes. I came close...but you saved me from that twice, but that's not why I'm asking you out tonight."

Call me foolish, but I believed him. Did I believe him because he was believable or because I wanted to? That was a question I wasn't prepared to answer at the moment. "Why are you asking me out then?"

"Because I want to see you. Why else would I ask you out?"

"I don't know. I know I'm not your type and—"

"You don't know anything about me that I haven't told you."

"Then tell me."

"I want to see you. Are you busy tonight or not?"

His brusque tone alone should have been enough to make me hang up on him. Instead I closed my eyes, shook my head, and then decided to follow my heart. Heart? Did I say heart? I meant inclination. At that point, my heart was not involved. That's what I wanted to avoid—getting my heart involved.

Wanting him physically was fine. Starting to feel anything *real* for a man who needed rescuing from sleeping with his brother's wife, was not. I should have told him to go to hell the moment he admitted he wanted Lea. But when I recalled the feel of his aroused body on mine...his cock lying between my thighs, his warm, insistent lips moving over my breasts and my lips, I couldn't. I wanted to feel the magic of knowing how easily I could arouse him again.

I won't deny that I also liked the idea that this big, handsome hunky man was pursuing me. Even if nothing came of going out with him again, just the thought of holding his attention for a few weeks was a real ego booster. As long as I didn't lose my head and delude myself into thinking anything real was happening between us, I should be fine. And I'd tell him I might be renewing my relationship with Darren so there would be no deception on my part. Not that he'd have any room to talk about deception with the way he'd been behaving with Lea. Surely both he and Lea were deceiving his brother.

I spoke slowly. "No. I'm not busy tonight."

"Great."

He sounded so relieved; I felt a gratified smile spreading across my face.

"Can I pick you up in an hour?"

"Make it 90 minutes and you've got a date–on one condition."

"Condition? Oh hell. I hate conditions."

"Don't we all?"

"What condition?"

"That you stay away from Lea."

A long silence followed.

As the seconds ticked away so did my hopes. He'd lied to me and now his lies were falling apart. "I guess that's a no, huh? You can't stay away from her?"

When he finally spoke, his voice was cold enough to send shivers down my spine. "You guess wrong. It's over between us."

For a moment, I thought he was saying it was over between us as in he and I. A wall of pain that shocked and frightened me rolled over me. I couldn't speak past a sudden lump in my throat. My eyes welled with tears.

"Lea is history."

I had to swallow several times as his meaning sank in. It was over between him and Lea—not he and I. It took several moments before I could trust myself to speak in a semi normal voice. "Are you sure? She seemed very interested in how our date went."

"It's over. She's out of my system. I haven't given her a single thought in the last five days. She's my brother's wife. I won't forget that again."

"You'd better not because if you think I want anything to do with a man capable of sleep—"

"I won't forget and I'll never go near her again. You have my word that it's over."

I wasn't sure at that point how good his word was, but I wanted to believe him. So I did. "Good."

"Okay. I'll see you soon, Bree."

My heart raced and I felt warm all over at the thought of seeing him again. That's when I should have known I'd allowed myself to feel more for him than I should.

I nodded. "Ah...okay."

Jake

I guess I should have known things could get out of hand with Bree, when I could barely wait to see her that night. But this time I was determined not to allow my lust to get out of control. Having said that, when she opened her door and smiled at me, I wrapped my arms around her and pressed a series of hot, hungry kisses against her lips.

They were so soft, sweet, and warm...so lush I couldn't stop kissing her until I felt her hands pressing against my shoulders. I lifted my lips a breath away from hers. "What?"

"Jake. I need to breath and you're holding me too tightly. Let go."

I sighed and released her. "Sorry."

She licked her lips and took a deep breath. "Whew. Someone is feeling a little horny, huh?"

I raked a hand through my hair. "You have that effect on me."

She placed a hand on my arm, staring up at me. "You're a very attractive man who can probably spend time with any woman you want."

I took her free hand in mine. "That's what I'm planning to do tonight with you."

She shook her head. "Why are you really here?"

Damn she was hard to convince. I squeezed the hand I held. "I'm here because I want to see you. For God's sake, Bree, why else would I be here?"

She shrugged. "Am I still a buffer between you and Lea?"

"No. No. I told you that's over. I'm here because I want to see you. Period. There's no hidden motive for you to ferret out. I want to see you tonight. Why is that so difficult for you to believe?"

"I don't want to be used because you can't have Lea."

"I don't want her anymore. I want you."

"So you're over her?"

"Yes."

"Just like that?"

"Yes."

"How?"

"Because I want you. That's how," I told her.

She moistened her lips. "You sound so...intense. For how long?"

"For how long?" Damn she was a great one for busting a man's balls. "What do you want from me? You want a contract? I don't know for how long. There are no guarantees in relationships, Bree."

"I know that, but if you ask to take me out, I don't want to have to wonder if I'm just a substitute for her."

I thought of the long legged blonde I'd slept with the previous Sunday night. She'd been pretty, sexy, and fairly good in bed. Yet the moment I'd recovered from my climax, I'd found myself wanting Bree. When she'd offered to spend the night with me, I'd taken her home instead. Then I'd spent the rest of the night thinking about Bree. Bree.

I couldn't get her out of my head. "I'm here tonight because you are the one—the only woman— I want to be with tonight."

"Just tonight? What about tomorrow or next week? Who are you going to want to be with then?"

What the hell? Could she read my damned mind? "Damn, you're tough. How about for the foreseeable future?"

She kept her gaze locked with mine for several moments before she smiled and stretched up to kiss my cheek. She stroked her fingers through the hair at my nape. "That'll do for now, Jake."

I closed my eyes briefly and sighed in relief. "Yeah?"

"Yeah." She smiled and kissed my cheek again. "So let's get the night started."

I should have known she wasn't going to let me off the hook that easily. Although she talked about music on the drive to dinner, she grilled me like a fillet as we ate. She asked about everything from where I went to school to how many lovers I'd had. I answered all her questions honestly. I didn't want any lies coming back to haunt me later.

Did that satisfy her? Hell no. Then she wanted to know how many of my lovers had been black.

I didn't really want to admit that Jess and I had once been lovers, but I didn't dare lie to her. If things went as I hoped, the two of them would meet one day and I knew Jess would tell her the truth. Better she hear it from me than Jess. "One."

She nodded. "How many were full-figured Plain-Janes?"

I sat back in my chair and gave her a cool look. There was no way I was going to admit I thought she was full-figured. Forget even hinting I thought she was plain because strangely enough, I no longer thought of her that way. True she wasn't beautiful—at least on the outside. But there was something so warm, sweet, and natural about her that shone from within that made it difficult to continue to think of her as plain.

Mom had always said there were different kinds of beauty. I'd never really believed her—until that moment. Sitting across the table from Bree and feeling that nameless something within her tugging at something within me, I think I began to believe that physical beauty was only skin deep.

Other kinds of beauty went much deeper and were lasting...more powerful. When Lea's outward beauty had long since faded, Bree's inner fire and warmth would be just as strong and vibrant as it was now. It would be just as attractive and impossible to resist as it was now.

"How many ways do I have to tell you? I'm where I want to be with the woman I want to be with. What part of that concept are you having trouble understanding? I'm where I want to be—with you. Is that plain enough?"

She shook her head. "I just want to understand what it is about me you find so...irresistible."

It was a fair question, but I didn't think she'd really want to hear me going on about inner fire and beauty, which would imply she had no outward or physical beauty worth mentioning. So I was not going there.

I wasn't sure what to say though. Did I again admit that I just wanted to be with her? Or did I admit when I thought about her it wasn't always in terms of sex anymore? I'm not saying I didn't still want to fuck her until she could barely walk because I did. But I also just wanted to be with her. I wanted to get to know her and be the man she turned to when she was lonely…afraid…horny…happy. I wanted to be there for her—period. That was a difficult concept to accept all at once.

I sighed. "Isn't it enough that I'm here because I want to be? Why does everything have to have an answer? Sometimes people are attracted to opposites."

"Sometimes?"

I nodded. "Sometimes…like now…with me and you."

She gave me a silent stare. I stared back. Have I told you she has the most beautiful, dark brown eyes I've ever seen? They kind of draw you so deep into their depths, you feel like you're drowning in bliss.

When she remained silent, I reached across the table and squeezed her left hand. "Of all the women I've ever known, and as I've just admitted, I've known a lot, you're the one I want to be with."

I saw something flick in her eyes before she spoke. "Really? You mean that?"

I nodded. "There's not one of them I'd rather be with than you. What more can I say?"

She gave me an unblinking stare. "You sound as if you mean that."

I nodded and squeezed her hand again. "I rarely feel the need to lie. I do mean it, Bree. I wouldn't trade tonight with you for a million nights with anyone else."

She smiled and her beautiful eyes softened, but being Bree, she had to rake me over the coals a little more. "Not even a super model type like Lea if she were available?"

I hesitated. Dare I admit that I'd had a one night stand after leaving her on Sunday? I shrugged and decided I didn't want any secrets between us. "I met one of those last Sunday when I...left you."

Chapter Eight

I watched her lips compress before she spoke. "And?"

"And I'm here with you instead of with her. What does that tell you?"

For a moment, I expected her to ask if I'd slept with her. Instead, she smiled again. Damn she has a beautiful smile. "That she's a lousy lover?"

I laughed. "What does it take to make a believer of you?"

"It's not that I don't believe you."

"Then why the third degree?"

"I just don't want to get...hurt."

"You think I want to hurt you?"

"I don't know." She sighed. "That's why this...thing with you is a little scary. I don't know what you want from me."

She seemed to want assurances I wasn't prepared to give. At that point, I was as uncertain and confused as she was. One moment I was enchanted by her inner warmth and the next I still thought getting over her would be easy–once I'd made love to her a few times.

It was difficult to believe that I'd ever thought she was in cahoots with Lea. She was as sweet and real as Lea was devious and hateful. "Hurting you is not on the list of things I'd like to do to and with you."

"So, you have a list, huh?"

I nodded.

"What's on it?"

I arched a brow. "Are you sure you want to know?"

She nodded. "I want to know where we stand with each other."

I had a feeling she wanted to know a lot more than that. And I wanted to tell her more. But I had a feeling she already knew I wanted to undress her and fuck her over and over again. I wasn't so sure she was in the mood to hear that. I shrugged. "I've told you. I want you. Period."

She tilted her head. "So? Was she?"

"Was who what?"

"Was your supermodel type a lousy lover?"

"My supermodel lover?" I released her hand and sat back in my chair. "What makes you think I slept with her?"

"Didn't you?"

Damn, she was tough. "Does it matter?"

"That depends."

"On?"

"Did you use protection?" She asked.

"If I had slept with her, it wouldn't have been without protection. I know the virtues of safe sex."

"And that's all you're going to say about your night with your supermodel?"

"No." I recaptured her hand. "I'll tell you that meeting her left me longing to see you again."

"Oh...Jake." She got a dreamy look on her face, and then shook her head. "Oh, no you don't, you silver-tongued devil. I want to know what happened between you two."

"I'm sure you do."

"Well? Tell me."

I shook my head and squeezed her hand. "When you and I are in an exclusive relationship, then you can give me the third degree and expect to get all your questions answered."

"When? Or if?"

I shrugged. "I don't have a crystal ball so I can't tell which one will be more applicable. I do know which I prefer though."

I watched her moisten her lips. "Really?"

I lifted her hand and rubbed it against my cheek. "Why don't we just see where this goes?"

"With or without benefits?"

"I think you know which I prefer." I brushed my lips against the back of her hand. "What about you? What's your preference?"

"I...ah...I don't know."

I released her hand and blew out a long breath. "I know I didn't exactly make a good impression last week in the park, but that will not happen again."

She tilted her head. "Really? You're assuming you're going to have another opportunity to—"

I narrowed my gaze. Damn I was tired of her jerking me around. "Yes. I am assuming that, Bree."

"Are you? Well, you'd better know we're not having another park episode."

I shook my head, annoyed that she kept harping on that. "Look, Bree—"

"No. You look, Jake. I'm not interested in a man who wants to bang me in public."

I raked a hand through my hair. "Don't make me sound like some...there was no one around. It's not as if we were performing before an audience and—"

"I have boundaries that I expect you to respect, Jake. Is that going to be a problem for you?"

Oh, she knew how to push my buttons—big time. "No, it's not going to be a problem."

"You're sure?"

"Yes. No more making out in public places. I promise."

"And when I say no, I mean no."

Oh, shit. She did feel as if I'd forced myself on her. "Look, Bree, I swear I never meant to force you or—"

"Force me?" She shook her head. "You didn't force yourself on me." She paused and narrowed her gaze. "If I'd felt like I was being raped, what was left of those big balls of yours would have a permanent imprint of my knee."

I sucked in a breath, annoyed by her words. Damn, but sometimes she pissed me off. "Then what the hell is your point, Bree?"

"That I only say no when I mean it."

The hell she did. If she thought I believed that, she was sadly mistaken. I suppressed an angry sigh that she seemed determined to bust my balls. "Most women have degrees of nos."

Her gaze narrowed. "Really? Well, when I say no, I mean it, Jake. No damned degrees. No means no. Is that clear?"

It wasn't. If she didn't feel as if I'd forced her, then didn't that mean she hadn't really meant no? Otherwise, wouldn't she have kneed me as she'd just threatened? I clearly wasn't the only one with issues.

But I wasn't about to point out her faulty reasoning. I nodded. "Crystal." I took her hand again. "And I am sorry. It won't happen again."

"It had better not."

"It won't." I squeezed her hand. "So are we all right now?"

She hesitated before she nodded. "I think so."

I felt such a relief that I should have known then that the tide had turned and there was no going back for me. "Great." I smiled and lifted her hand to my lips. "Let's celebrate with a dance."

"What are we celebrating?"

"You and me being friends with benefits."

She turned a sweet, sexy smile on me that made me want to melt. "Okay."

I felt like a teenager holding her hand as we walked onto the dance floor. I could hardly wait to turn and take her into my arms. Dancing close with her was sweet torture. Feeling her large breasts and thighs against me nearly drove me into a sexual frenzy. I wanted to take her back to the table and fuck her until I was limp and sore. But this time I was going to show her that I could control myself.

I was determined to show her I could be considerate of her needs and feelings and put them before my own. There would be no slam, bam, thank you, ma'am, this time. No more premature explosions that left her frustrated.

As we danced, it was my turn to ask her about the men in her life.

She sighed. "I don't think I've ever really been in love."

"But?"

She spoke after a very noticeable pause. "Well...there was someone who was fairly...special."

I felt my jaw clenching and took a moment to control a wave of panic. "How special? Were you lovers?"

"Yes. We were."

"What happened?"

"Our relationship ended when he moved to California."

Lucky day for me.

She paused again and then spoke in a rush. "Just so you know, he called me tonight. He...he's planning to come back to Philly for a visit in a few weeks."

Oh, hell, I didn't like the sound of that. "And?"

She shrugged. "And I just want to be upfront with you."

This shit was sounding worse all the time. "What's to be upfront about? You said the relationship was over. It is over. Isn't it?"

"Yes, it is."

"But?"

"But nothing."

"You still care about him?"

"I still like him, but I don't sleep with more than one man at a time."

"And that's it?"

"There's nothing else to say, Jake. Our sexual relationship ended when he left for California."

Then why did I feel as if she weren't being straight with me? "Why is he coming back? He wants back in your bed. Doesn't he?"

There was another damned pause before she spoke. "He...we have talked about that possibility...but..."

I struggled to keep my tone even. "But what?"

"How many times do I have to say I don't sleep with more than one man at a time?"

How the hell was that statement supposed to make me feel better about her ex-lover coming back into her life for one thing—sex? "Since you're not sleeping with me, that's not a lot of comfort, Bree. You're planning to sleep with him again. Aren't you?"

"Jake—"

"Don't Jake me, Bree. Tell me something to make his coming okay."

She lifted her head and stared up at me. "I already have. I don't sleep with two men at the same time."

I compressed my lips. There was no point in reminding her she and I weren't lovers. So what was going to prevent her from hoping into bed with this ex she still had feelings for?

She ran her hands over my chest. "Okay?"

Okay? Hell no, it wasn't okay, but I thought it better not to admit that. To keep her from sleeping with him again, I had to ensure she and I were sleeping together by the time he arrived in town. So much for my half-formed plan to show her I could wait for sex. Hell would freeze over before I let this stupid ass get his hands on her again. He'd blown his chance with her and I'd be damned if I'd allow him anywhere near her bed ever again.

If he wanted a damned casual fuck, he'd better look somewhere else. Bree was off limits to him. I would need to get her into bed as soon as possible. Get her in bed and keep her there. I'd wine and dine her for a week and then come hell or high water, she and I were going to be lovers. And when this ex brought his sorry ass back to Philly, I'd make sure he knew Bree now belonged to me.

She tugged at my lapel. "Jake? Is it okay?"

I stared at her. "Yes. It's okay—as long as you realize there's no way in hell I'm going to stand by and allow you to sleep with him or anyone else, Bree. If you think..." I stopped and sucked in an angry breath. Why the hell had I allowed her to see how I felt? Now, womanlike, when she got the opportunity, she'd use my admission against me. "I'm sorry. I...I didn't mean that."

"Didn't you, Jake?"

"No."

She clearly wasn't fooled. "Okay, Jake. You didn't mean it." She smiled and pressed her cheek against my shoulder again.

Shit. I was toast now.

"Don't worry, Jake. I have a feeling everything is going to be okay now."

I had no idea what the hell she was hinting at, but I didn't care. I had a plan to ensure her ex remained that way. I tightened my arms and continued slow dancing with her.

At ten-thirty, she sighed and lifted her head from my shoulder. "It's getting late and tomorrow's going to be a busy day."

I gazed down into her eyes. "Are you tired?"

"A little and it's late."

I decided not to point out that the following day was Saturday and she could sleep as late as she liked. "Okay. I'll take you home."

She seemed surprised, but nodded. I think she was expecting me to make a nuisance of myself. But I was determined to be on my best behavior. I held her hand on the short walk to my car. After I opened the passenger door, I resisted the urge to force her to brush against me to get inside.

On the drive to her apartment, she told her about her day at work. I was highly relieved when she didn't mention Lea. The sooner she forgot how big an ass I'd been with Lea, the better.

At her apartment door, even though I wanted to kiss her senseless, I contented myself with a few hungry kisses before I released her. Or should I say I stopped kissing her. Although I kept my tongue in my mouth, I was still cupping her large ass. I loved the feel of her breasts against my chest. And her ass. Damn, I loved holding and touching it. There's no doubt I wanted to fuck her, but I liked holding her too. There was something about her that made me feel an inner peace and happiness I'd never experienced with anyone else. And that was a little scary because she was not my type.

But judging by the way I was feeling, she might be the woman who changed my type. If that were true, I'd deal with it later. At the moment, I needed to keep my cool.

Hopefully she'd finally be ready for a fuck on Thursday. That would be about as long as I could stand to wait to get her in bed. I kissed her cheek, near the corner of her sweet, soft, addictive lips. "Are you going to be busy on Thursday?"

She shook her head and muzzled my cheek. "Ah...Thursday...ah....no."

She sounded surprised. She was probably wondering why I wasn't asking her out over the weekend. I wanted to, but this time, I wanted to take things slow.

I licked her lips. "Have dinner with me on Thursday?"

"Ah...what...ah...yes."

I kissed her lips and released her. "Six o'clock?"

To my surprise, she slipped her arms around my neck, leaned into me, and pressed those sweet lips of hers against mine in a long, delicious kiss that made my cock rock hard. "Yes." She licked my bottom lip and stepped away from me, a sexy smile on her lips. "Good night."

Good night instead of goodbye? Yes. You know you have it bad when you leave a woman with blue balls and yet feel like you've won the lottery just because she said good night instead of goodbye.

I watched her go inside and then listened to her lock the door before I walked away from her with a big grin on my face. For the first time since Lea had dumped me, my romantic future looked promising again. So Bree wasn't a beauty on the outside, but she had other qualities in abundance that more than compensated for any mere lack of physical beauty.

And really, it wasn't as if Bree were unattractive. She was far from that. She had the most incredible smile, a sex appeal I couldn't resist, and a way of making me feel like the luckiest man in the world because I was with her. What more could a man want from a woman or a relationship? What was so called beauty when compared to her other considerable charms?

If I lost my sight, I'd no longer be able to appreciate physical beauty, but I'd still be able to feel the warmth and fire in Bree that was slowly drawing me to her in a way no other woman ever had.

Still, for all my new found "feelings," and determination to give her at least a few days before I gave into lust I only got half way home before I knew I was not going to be able to sleep that night unless I got laid. I briefly considered my options. It was rather gratifying that Lea was nowhere on the list of "options" for satisfying my sexual hunger. Thanks to Bree, the madness of being drawn to or wanting Lea was history. So what did that leave? I thought of the long-legged blonde, but only briefly. I didn't really want to sleep with her again and if Bree found out later, such a lapse might create a real problem between us. But I still had needs that ate at me. And what the hell was I supposed to do about them?

Chapter Nine

Bree

After Jake left, I felt restless and needy. I undressed and took my favorite sex toy to bed with me. Thinking of Jake and recalling the feel of his arms around me as we danced earlier and the feel of his lips as we kissed goodnight, I closed my eyes. I pretended I was with him. But I wasn't and my body knew it. Half an hour later, I lay still trying to buzz myself to a climax. It wasn't working. I turned off the vibrator and rolled onto my stomach.

I would get up and shower. While I did, I'd train a steady spray of water from the removable showerhead on my clit. That had never failed to make me come.

I slipped out of bed and headed for the bathroom. The phone rang before I reached the door. I went back to the nightstand to answer it. It was Jake. "Jake? What's wrong?" I frowned. Was he about to sleep with Lea again? If he was, this time I just might let him. Damned if I were going to let him use me to stay out of his sister-in-law's bed. I shouldn't need to do that. His damned conscience should be enough to ensure he didn't sleep with her.

Just the thought that he might want to sleep with her again after all the assurances he'd given me during dinner, made me snappish. "Do you need your bacon pulled out of the fire again? Because if you do—"

"If you mean am I about to sleep with Lea, the answer's not just no, but hell no. That ship has sailed and it's never coming back to this port again."

"No?"

"No."

He sounded as if he meant it and that was such a relief. "Then what's the problem?"

"The problem is that I have needs."

"Yeah? What kind?"

"I'm not in the mood for games, Bree. You know what I mean and you know what I want and who I want it from—you."

Boy did I know the feeling, but just then I needed to get to that showerhead. "Well, maybe we can talk about it Thursday. I'm not making any promises, but maybe we could—"

"That's nice, but that's not going to help me now. And I need help from you now."

"Meaning?"

"I mean I need you now. Tonight."

"Tonight? I...I..."

"Please, Bree. Don't torture me. I can't wait until Thursday."

I swallowed several times. "All right. Maybe we can have dinner on Tuesday instead."

"No. That's not going to work for me either. That's too long."

"What did you have in mind?"

"I'm in your lobby now. Buzz me in."

I closed my eyes. I wanted him, but did I want him enough to sleep with him that night? My pussy pulsed and I had my answer. I opened my eyes and tossed my toy into my nightstand drawer.

"Bree? Are you still there?"

"Yes."

"Buzz me in."

I bit my lip. Tonight hadn't been our first or second date, but I'd only known him a week. Did I want to sleep with a man I'd only known for a week? Granted, it seemed a much longer time, but—

"Bree? Please. Buzz me in."

I buzzed him in from the lobby. Then I went to my closet and pulled out the white teddy hanging there.

I stared at my reflection. What if he thought my breasts were too large for the almost nonexistent bra support provided by the teddy? I stroked a hand over my belly. What if—

My apartment doorbell rang. I took a deep breath and went to the door. "Yes?"

"It's me."

It was now or never. I decided I wanted it to be now. I opened the door.

He stared at me for so long in silence I wished I'd never bought the damned teddy. That is until he finally spoke. Then I thought buying it was the best move I'd never made.

"Holy hell, Bree."

My body is far from perfect. My breasts are large, but they sag. My stomach isn't flat. My ass is just plain big. I'm no beauty by any stretch of the imagination, but just hearing those three words, spoken in that low, awed voice, made me feel like the sexiest woman alive.

I licked my lips and smiled at him. "Do you like my new teddy?"

"Like it? Like isn't the word."

"It isn't?"

"Damn, woman, you look good in white lace." He reached out and brushed his hand against my breasts. "But I'm betting you'll look even better stark naked."

Maybe so, but I wasn't about to strip. I didn't feel comfortable enough with my body to allow him to see me naked. I took his hand and pulled him inside. I closed and locked the door before I turned to face him. By that time, he'd already kicked off his shoes. His jacket and tie were in a pile on the floor.

I rubbed my pussy. "You're overdressed."

"Give me a moment."

He practically tore off the rest of his clothes, keeping his gaze on my breasts the entire time. That made me feel a little self-conscious, but also kind of sexy.

He stripped down to his underwear. I leaned against the door, allowing my gaze to linger on the bulge in his briefs. When he was fully aroused, I was going to close my eyes, and savor the delight of feeling him sliding slowly inside my body. Or maybe I'd watch his big cock going inside my pussy before I closed my eyes. Whichever one I decided, I'd have to get him hard first.

I pushed away from the door and closed the distance between us. Lifting my chin and parting my lips, I slid my hands down his chest, over his six-pack abs, and into the waistband of his briefs. I closed one hand over his balls and cupped the other one over his semi-hard flesh.

It seemed like an age since I'd held a real cock. I closed my eyes briefly and just savored the delight of holding his cock and balls for several moments before I needed more. I lifted his cock and balls out of his briefs and stared down at them.

I love a man with big, hairy balls and an even bigger cock. I stared up at him and felt a chill down to my toes. I saw desire in his gaze. There was also a tenderness I'd never expected to see in his eyes. That look scared the hell out of me.

I released him and turned away, shaking. Afraid.

"Bree? What's wrong?"

I shook my head. "Nothing. I just don't think I'm ready for this yet." I wrapped my arms around my body and waited for the explosion of anger I knew was coming and knew I deserved. I half expected him to force me. If he did, part of me wouldn't have blamed him too much–not after having pushed him so far.

When his hands closed over my shoulders, I tensed, trying to prepare myself for what was coming. I was not prepared for what actually happened. He turned me to face him. I kept my gaze downward, but then I was looking at him genitals. I didn't want that so I closed my eyes.

He caressed my cheek. "Bree? What's wrong?"

"Nothing. I'm just not ready to sleep with you yet."

He lifted my chin. "Open your eyes."

"No, I—"

"Open your eyes."

I did and to my surprise, there was none of the anger in his gaze I expected or deserved. He caressed my cheek again. "What's wrong?"

His voice was soft and soothing and I found myself admitting how I felt. "I...I'm afraid."

"Of what?"

"Of the look in your eyes...how it makes me feel."

"So you don't want to have sex after all?"

"I do...but I don't. I'm not ready to sleep with you."

He closed his eyes and blew out a breath. "Are you sure?"

"Yes."

He released me, stepped back, and pulled his briefs up over his cock and balls. "Fine."

I watched as he quickly dressed in silence.

I sighed. "Go ahead. I know I deserve it so say it."

He pulled on his jacket. "Good night." He pulled the door open.

I had a feeling that if I let him leave, I'd never see him again. "Jake. Wait."

He paused, but didn't turn to face me. "What?"

"I'm sorry."

He pressed his forehead against the open door and then turned to face me. "Why do you keep doing this to me, Bree?"

I heard the desperation in his voice and felt bad and afraid I'd blown it with him. "I...I'm sorry."

"The hell you are." He suddenly slammed the door shut and stared at me. "You love jerking me around. Why don't you just admit it?"

"I don't."

"Then why the hell come to the door half-naked, get me hot and aroused, and then say you're not ready for sex?"

I bit my lip. "I don't usually sleep around so early in a relationship and—"

"And I don't want to hear that shit."

"Jake."

"Don't Jake me, Bree. You knew you wanted to wait longer when you came to the door dressed like that."

I've never been one of those women who cry easily, but I felt kind of weepy because although he was angry, he wasn't nearly as angry as he had a right to be.

"I'm feeling very confused. Can we just...can you just hold me?"

"What? I have blue balls, which you gave me and now you just what me to hold you?"

I nodded. "Yes."

He stared at me, his gaze as cold as dry ice. "Are you nuts?"

I opened my arms. "Hold me?"

"Woman, you are certifiable." He pushed himself away from the door and stopped a foot or so from me. "You want to be held with no sex?"

I nodded.

He extended an arm. "Fine. Bring your big, round ass over here."

"I don't want sex."

"I said come here."

I shook my head.

"I've taken all the shit tonight I intend to take from you, Bree. Get your big ass over here."

I pressed a hand against my pounding heart. "Jake."

"Don't make me tell you again."

I took several deep breaths and obeyed him.

He closed his hands over my shoulders and glared down at me. "You little tease. I should spank your ass until you can't sit down for a week."

"Jake, I—"

"Shut the fuck up."

I blinked up at him. He looked and sounded so angry. For the first time, I wondered if I needed to fear him.

He jerked at my shoulders and pulled my body against his.

I felt the tension in him and trembled.

He put his arms around me and raked his teeth against my ear. "If you need to be held...hell, I'll hold you...all damn night."

I nearly drowned in a wave of relief. Anger quickly followed. I lifted my head and looked at him. "I was afraid of you for a moment."

He arched a brow. "Were you?"

Noting the lack of remorse in his gaze, I frowned. "You deliberately frightened me, Jake."

"So?"

"So? You admit it?"

"Yes, I do. You had it coming."

I jerked away from him. "Bastard."

He reached out and jerked me back against him. "Don't bastard me, Bree. If you were with a man who cared less, you'd have reason to be afraid."

"And you think your anger makes frightening me acceptable?"

"Do you think your fear of what you thought you saw in my eyes made it all right for you to jerk my chain again? You came to the door half-naked. You told me I was overdressed. You had your greedy little hands all over my cock and balls. Then you tell me you don't want sex and expect me to play nice? What the fuck is your problem, woman?"

"Jake."

He tightened his hands on my shoulders. "Shut up, Bree."

I swallowed a rush of angry, hurtful words and glared at him.

"Any other man would drag you into the bedroom, fling you on your bed with your legs open, and fuck you hard—until he'd had his fill of you."

I sucked in a hurt breath at his harsh words. I would never forgive him for that half threat.

His blue eyes softened and he lifted a hand to caress my cheek. His next words dissolved my anger and hurt as if they'd never existed. "But there's not enough money in the world to make me treat you that way. I wouldn't hurt you for anything and I'm sorry I scared you."

He drew me against his chest and wrapped his arms around me. "If you need to be held, I want to be the man who holds you."

I pressed my cheek against his shoulder. "No sex?"

He sighed. "It will probably kill me, but no sex." He kissed my cheek and slapped my ass hard.

I didn't protest. I was just too happy and thankful that he was still there, although he was rightfully annoyed.

He slipped his hands down my body to palm my ass. He caressed both cheeks.

I shivered and pressed closer.

"Which way to your bedroom?"

I pulled away from him and took his hand. I led him to my bedroom. He stripped down to his briefs, I turned on my CD clock radio to my favorite jazz station, and we got into bed. I turned on my side. He turned off the light, curled his body behind me, and slipped an arm around me. His palm settled over my breast.

I trembled. "You said no sex."

He nibbled at my ear. "But I didn't say I wouldn't touch or caress you. If my touching you makes you change your mind, I'm not going to complain." He slowly ground his groin against my ass and I felt his cock. He was still semi-erect. So clearly he was still aroused. And now strangely enough, so was I.

I moved his hand from my breasts and placed it between my legs.

He's a bright boy. He immediately found the opening in the teddy and slipped his fingers inside my pussy.

I licked my lips and rotated my ass against him. "Hmmm."

He licked the side of my neck and began finger fucking me. "Your pussy is very wet." He blew into my ear. "It's so slick...a pussy this wet and slick needs a big, hard cock inside it. Don't you think?"

My stomach muscles clenched, my heart raced, and I was so hungry for him I couldn't pretend I didn't want him. "Yes," I whispered and turned in his arms to face him. "Yes...I need a cock inside me."

"A cock?"

The only light in the room was the moonlight shining through the partly opened curtains. I shook my head and caressed his face. "Your cock."

"That's what I needed to hear."

He sounded so happy and satisfied I knew the time was right to give myself to him. I could worry about the consequences later. At that moment, I had to have him between my legs....on top of me...inside me...

He kissed me. It was a soft, gentle kiss that touched something far more special than just my sexual desire. I had expected passion from him but not tenderness. That made me feel more vulnerable and a little more afraid. This time I knew there could be no turning back. I was amazed I'd ever found the strength to resist him. I wanted sex with him and I wanted it now.

I slipped one arm around his neck and reached down with my other hand to cup his cock. It was so hard and heavy. I hungered to finally feel it inside me...loving me...fucking me into an oblivious, delirious haze of delight.

He made a small sound against my lips. He has the warmest, sweetest lips I've ever tasted. I kissed him back, rubbing my breasts against his chest.

He groaned and rolled me onto my back. I parted my legs and tilted my hips so my aching, empty pussy was in the right position to welcome his cock. He settled against me and I felt the length of his cock against my slit. He felt warm and pulsing. What an incredible feeling. What delights I was about to experience?

He seemed inclined to just linger like that. But I had needs and other ideas about what he should do with that long cock of his. I rubbed my pussy against him, telling him without words that I wanted and needed him inside me.

I was hot and ready to be fucked-hard, but he took his time. He deepened his kiss as he caressed me. I felt as if his palm was burning its heat right through the teddy, past my skin, and onto my nerve endings. His touch along with his warm, insistent kisses heightened my desire. My cunt flooded and I had to have him.

I moaned against his lips and wantonly rubbed my pussy against his cock. *This pussy is yours to do with as you like, baby. Take me...take it. Fuck us both.*

He lifted his lips from mine. "Have you changed your mind about no sex? If you haven't, you're going to have to stop rubbing against my cock right now or else."

Chapter Ten

Bree

Okay, so maybe he wasn't as bright as I'd thought he was. Later, I appreciated his consideration in allowing me one last chance to say no. But in the heat of lust and need, I just wanted his cock in me. I decided to make it clear, that for the moment, at least, all my doubts had been resolved. I knew what I wanted and needed and he was the man I wanted it from. I clutched his ass. "I want you and your cock," I told him in a shameless, needy voice. "Put on a condom and fuck me...ride me long, hard, and deep."

"A condom?"

"Yes, yes, a condom," I spoke impatiently. "Put one on and fuck me, Jake."

"I'm going to fuck you all right, but not with a condom."

I needed him so badly, it was difficult to think clearly. I blinked up at him, confused. "Not with a....what...?"

"To hell with a condom."

"What?"

"I feel like I've waited an eternity for this moment with you. Now that you're ready to admit you and your pussy belong exclusively to me, I want to fully enjoy fucking the hell out of you."

He wanted me all to himself. I liked the idea, but when had we talked about exclusivity? "Jake…"

He lifted off me, gripped his cock, and pressed it against my cunt. "I want your bare pussy right now."

"Jake. Wait."

"For what? Don't you know what's going on between us by now?"

"No."

"Then I'll make it clear. I want—I need to fuck you—with nothing between us. If you don't want that, say so right now because I'm not in the mood to play any more games with you."

"Games?" That stung. I knew I'd been far more indecisive with him than I normally was. But then I'd never fallen so hard for someone like him. "You think I've been playing games with you?"

He made an impatient sound. "I don't care what you call it, that's how it's felt."

"Jake. We've only known each other—"

"I know how long we've know each other. And I know something else, as well. I'm fucking you without protection."

"And if I object?"

"I'll leave."

I parted my lips.

He shook his head, his gaze narrowing. "Before you speak you should know that if I leave now, I won't be back."

Charming. Either I behaved like an irresponsible teenager and let him fuck me without protection or he'd walk out of my life for good. I've never liked being threatened. I should have kicked his tight ass out of my bed, but I was almost beyond rational thought. Even though I didn't realize it until later, I was in love with him and wanted to please him—at any cost.

I did the only thing I could, given the circumstances and my feelings for him. I capitulated. But I had to make one thing crystal clear to him. "I'm allergic to the pill," I warned.

He caressed my wet slit. "There are other methods of birth control."

"Yes. One is called a condom," I pointed out. "You might have heard of them. Responsible men use them all the time."

"I'm responsible and I use them too." He slipped a finger in my pussy. "Not with you. Using one with you doesn't feel right. I want to feel your pussy surrounding and cradling my cock when we both come. I want to come inside you."

"I could end up pregnant."

"If you do, we'll be parents in nine months."

"What if I don't want to be a mother that soon?"

"Then you shouldn't allow horny men anywhere near this pretty pink, fragrant pussy of yours."

Pretty, pink, fragrant pussy? I'm a sucker for a man with a big cock who knows how to stroke the right buttons and make me feel sexy and irresistible. I closed my eyes and thrust my hips upwards. "I'm yours, Jake."

"Damn right you are."

"Fuck me."

He pushed down and oh, God, I felt the big head of his hard, bare cock parting the lips of my slit. Then he was inside me. Darren had been a skillful lover and sex with him had been beyond good, but that first, sweet slide of Jake's cock into me was the most incredible experience of my life. He was so hard and thick. As I felt him sliding deeper and deeper, his hard cock tunneling into my depths and stretching my pussy, I thought I would lose my mind. I couldn't think...just feel and react to the sweet delight we were sharing.

"Oh, hell, yeah." I moaned when he bottomed out in me. "Yeah."

He slowly ground his hips against me, so that I felt every inch of his hard, thick cock pulsing in me. What an utterly wonderful experience.

"Oh, damn, Bree, your pussy feels so good. It's so tight, hot, and slick."

He was holding that big, thick cock of his still. That wasn't working for me. I needed to feel it plunging deep and deeper still inside me. I curled my fingers in his hair. "Stop talking and fuck me."

"Oh, no." He nibbled at my lips. "No fucking. Not for our first time." He cupped my face between his palms and stared down at me. "I want our first time to be very special for you."

I swallowed a lump of emotion and stared silently up at him, probably falling a little more in love with him. Not that I was ready to admit it at that time.

"You're a sweet, sexy woman who deserves more than just a fuck. I'm going to make love to you this time. I want to enjoy this sweet pussy of yours for as long as possible before I fill it up with my cum. We can fuck later."

I felt as if he made love to me with his sweet, romantic words. I was ready to melt and whatever little piece of my heart he didn't already own, became his.

I closed my eyes to hide a sudden rush of tears. "Oh, Jake."

He settled his hips against mine and gently kissed me as he slowly slid his hard cock in and out of me. Each time he sank that big, sweet cock of his deep into my pussy, he rubbed his chest against my breasts, and pressed a sweet, long kiss against my lips.

It's hard to describe how wonderful and sweet our first time together was for me. There was pleasure in abundance—more than I'd ever had with any other lover. But the deep, leisurely strokes of his cock, stirred other emotions that weren't physical. I felt as if he were making love to all of me and not just my body. As he loved me, I felt warm, cherished, and adored.

Even as my body threatened to catch fire with passion and desire, I felt as if he were capturing my heart, mind, and soul, with each deep, sweet foray into me. Each movement of his cock felt like a balm to my aching pussy. He made love to it...healed it...and totally conquered it.

His mouth and tongue singed my breasts and my lips. I felt as if I were lost in a world of unbridled passion and love. A knot of white-hot fire ignited in my belly. Sex had never been this good...this sweet...this utterly soul-destroying...this delicious.

I could feel the need for a glorious release building in my belly and spreading down to the pussy so full of his wonderful cock. I moaned softly against his demanding lips, ground my lips against his, and clutched at his hard ass. I wanted...I needed more cock...dear God, I needed it so badly.

He responded by pushing his hips downward, driving that wonderful cock of his as deep into my wet pussy as he could get it. The flame in my belly spread through my body.

He gripped my waist and rotating his powerful hips, he thrust in and out of me...driving me nearly insane with pleasure. It was too much. I couldn't hold back my climax. As he thrust his cock into me again, I sobbed and shuddered as my pussy caught fire.

"That's it, Bree. Come for me...let me feel that sweet, hot pussy juice of yours flowing all over my cock. Come all over my cock, baby."

Drowning in red-hot, lust and love, I arched my body into his, dug my nails into his ass, curled my toes, and I sobbed against his lips as I came all over his thrusting cock.

He slipped his tongue into my mouth and continued to fuck me through my climax. He wrapped his arms around me and laid his full weight on me. He started to thrust hard...deep and hard—just as I loved it. Hard and so deep, I could barely breathe from the pleasure slicing through my cunt and all through my body. He felt so good, I was a breath away from coming again when he groaned, bit into my bottom lip, and exploded inside me.

I held him close, with my hands clenched over his tight ass. Knowing he was shooting jet after jet of cum deep into my unprotected pussy was such a turn on.

He seemed to come for a long time. His seed was thick and copious and I loved each new blast into my body. Finally, he dragged his mouth away from mine and collapsed on top of me, his cock still buried deep in me.

I lay under him. Although I felt crushed, with a sated pussy full of cum and cock, I wasn't complaining.

After several minutes, he finally rolled us both onto our sides, and endeared himself to me by reaching between our bodies and rubbing my clit and finger fucking me until I came again.

Oh, damn, what a sweet, sweet lover.

By the time I'd come again, he was rock hard. I sighed happily when he slipped behind me, lifted my top leg, and thrust his big cock balls deep into my pussy.

My toes curled and I shuddered and moaned with pleasure. "I'm a mess," I protested. And I was tired. I yawned. "I should get up and shower."

He tightened his arm around my waist. "Your pussy is a lovely mess...yours and mine. You're not showering and washing our lovely mess away just yet."

I didn't argue.

He gently slid his cock in and out of me. "I love how your pussy feels full of my cum."

"I like it too," I admitted.

He rewarded me with a sharp, delicious slap on the side of my ass. "I think I'll spend the night with my cock buried in your tight, sweet pussy."

I liked the sound of the sexy threat. So I pushed my hips back, so that his cock slid in deeper. God, he has such a wonderful, addictive cock. There's good cock, as in Darren's cock, and then there's Jake's big sausage, in a class all by itself—just like the big, handsome man who wields it.

He sighed and cupped a hand over my breasts. "Damn, Bree, you are so hot, sexy, and sweet."

I smiled, pleased. "Hmmm. You like my pussy?"

"Like it?" He nibbled at my neck. "I love it. I might never remove my cock."

I reached down between our legs and cupped a hand over his balls, which rested just below my cunt. "I might never let you."

"I think we have a deal," he whispered, gently pinching my nipples.

"Yes. I think we do." I sighed happily and pushed my ass against his groin.

"But next time we fuck I want you totally naked."

I shivered. I wasn't sure I was ready to allow him to see my imperfect body.

He kissed the side of my neck. "I love your pussy, but that was too good to be just sex."

His words surprised and pleased me. I felt the same way, but was still a little afraid to explore our relationship beyond sex. "Oh, Jake."

He stroked my clit. "Now aren't you glad we made love instead of just holding each other?"

"Yes," I admitted.

"That's my woman." He withdrew his cock slightly and I felt a steady stream of his seed trickle out.

"Jake? I can feel your cum trickling down my ass. You must have shot a small ocean in me."

He sucked my neck. "You have the sweetest pussy I've ever fucked. You made me so horny and then you satisfied me so sweetly, I couldn't stop coming."

Damn, has he got a silver tongue or what? Even as I smiled, I felt sure that with all that cum inside me, it would be a miracle if I didn't end up pregnant.

"Give me a goodnight kiss."

I turned my head and he pressed a long, warm kiss against my lips.

When he finally lifted his head, I settled my ass against his groin and drifted to sleep with him still inside me. Can you say very nice?

Several hours later, I crawled out of his arms and the bed, and stumbled into the bathroom. Halfway there, I had to cup a hand over my pussy as I felt fluids seeping out of me through the vaginal hole in my teddy.

Before I left the bathroom, I wet and soaped up a washcloth to clean my pussy. I briefly considered removing the teddy, but decided to keep it on. If we had more than this one night, I'd need to allow him to see me naked, but for now...I wasn't ready.

I returned to the bedroom, wiggled back into his arms, kissed his slightly parted mouth.

I couldn't ever remember feeling so content after sex. Darren had never left me dissatisfied and I'd always felt as if he cared for me and wanted more than sex from me. Yet I'd never experienced this level of delight after sex.

There was something about Jake and knowing how much he'd wanted me that made sex with him more powerful and compelling than sex with any other man. Or maybe I was just in love for the first time, which probably explained why everything seemed so much sweeter and special with him. Either way, I didn't want the night with him to end. I would have been happy to lay there awake, basking in the glow of being in his arms for the rest of eternity. I fell asleep instead.

I woke the next morning to feel a pair of warm lips nibbling at mine. I opened my eyes. Jake lay on the bed beside me, smiling. His unshaven face is so handsome. I couldn't believe I was actually lying in bed with him.

He caressed my cheek. "Hi."

Gazing into his beautiful blue eyes, reality returned. Remembering how irresponsible I'd behaved the night before I finally knew how women who should have known better "found" themselves "unexpectedly" pregnant. I'd allowed him to come inside me. I needed to get my butt up and call my doctor to see about a morning after prescription. Or was it now over the counter? I couldn't remember. Don't misunderstand. I wanted at least one child, but not until I was happily married. I didn't want to get pregnant as a result of a one-night stand—no matter how mind blowing it had been.

"Hi." I moistened my lips. "I should get up and…"

He shook his head and urged me onto my back. "Not yet."

"Jake—"

"Shhh." He rose over me. Sliding between my legs, he thrust his cock deep into me.

I gasped, shuddered, and unable to resist him, I clutched him to me. "Dear, Lord, Jake, your cock feels so good."

He laughed softly and pressed his chest against my breasts. "I'm glad you like it so much."

I stared up at him, realizing for the first time that I was stark naked. How had he managed to undress me without waking me up? And how long had he been staring at my naked body?

"I'm naked."

"Yes you are—finally I have you the way I want you…naked, horny, in my arms and filled with my cock."

"Is this how you want me, Jake?"

"Oh, yeah, baby. Can't you tell?"

He sounded so sincere, I believed him. Besides, he'd already been staring at my nude body while I slept and he was still there. More importantly, his cock was hard as a rock and deep in my pussy. I stroked my hands down his back. "I love how good your cock feels inside me..."

"But?"

"But we should use a condom this time."

He arched a brow. "You think we should?"

"Oh, yes. Definitely. We need to use a condom." Even as I spoke, I rolled us over so that I was on top of him. I ground my pussy around his cock. Oh, damn, that felt good. I shuddered and caught my breath before I could speak in a relatively normal voice. "You must have pumped a river of cum in me last night."

He cupped his warm palms over my ass and grinned up at me. "Damn, our first time making love was good. Wasn't it?"

"Oh, hell, Jake, it was beyond good."

"It was beyond good." He slapped my ass. "So we're going to use a condom this time?"

"Yes." I bit my lip and rotated my hips, feeling every inch of his hard cock pulsing in me. The man's cock was a weapon and sweet beyond words. I sucked in a breath and cupped my hands over my breasts. "Yes."

I expected him to protest. Instead, he nodded. "Fine. Climb off my cock and I'll get one out of my wallet."

I blinked down at him, in a lust-filled haze. "What? What did you say? You expect me to get off your cock?"

He arched a brow. "I can't very well put on a condom with you sitting on my cock like this, can I? If you want me to use a condom, climb off. I'll be very quick. Before you know it, I'll have it on and be back inside your delicious, tight pussy."

His words got me even hotter. This cock...his cock was mine and damned if I weren't going to fully enjoy it. I lifted my hips until only the big head of his luscious cock remained inside my cunt. Instead of climbing off him, I plunged my hips down on his, forcing his cock back up into me. The jolt of pleasure I felt slamming myself down on him like that was so strong I nearly got light headed.

He groaned and I shuddered. "You had your chance. Now this unprotected pussy is mine for the plundering." He gripped my hips.

I was too impatient. I lifted my hips and pushed them down again. I lost all desire but one. Moaning and pinching my nipples, I began fucking myself on and off his thick cock.

He tightened his grip on my hips and held them still. "Bree, I can't put on a condom while you're fucking me."

"I know that," I moaned, still fucking him.

"I'm not pulling out," he warned in a brusque voice.

I was too far gone to think rationally. All I knew is I wanted his cock. He seemed to still retain the ability to think. Damn him.

Resisting my efforts to keep his cock buried deep in my pussy, he lifted my hips until only half his cock remained in my body. "If you're determined to use a condom, we have to stop now, while I still have a little control."

"We'll use one next time," I groaned and propelled myself down onto his thickness. I felt his pubic hair against mine and lost it. I rode him hard. Within seconds, shivers of pleasure started racing up and down my spine as my pussy caught fire.

"Next time hell," he groaned. "And it's time you realized who's fucking who here. You're my woman and I'll do the fucking, Bree."

I continued bouncing up and down on him until he rolled me onto my back. He rested his weight on his extended arms and stared down at me. "It's too late to expect me to ever use a condom. You're mine and this is my pussy. Mine." He thrust into me so hard, my toes curled.

"I'll fuck it and you as often as I want. There's never going to be a condom between your pussy and my cock. This is the way making love was supposed to be...no birth control and no condom between a man and his woman's pussy. I'm going to fuck you now—hard and deep."

I gasped up at him. "Oh...Jake..."

His eyes blazed down at me. "If we're lucky, you'll get pregnant and we'll have a baby together. When your belly swells as my baby grows inside you, everyone will know you're my woman. Your damned ex is going to stay your ex. He had his chance. He'd better keep his ass in L.A. if he doesn't want me to kick it back there. Now you're mine and I'm keeping you. You and this pussy belong exclusively to me now. You're all mine, baby."

Chapter Eleven

Bree

His hot, lustful words washed over me like a warm wave. At that moment I had everything in the world I wanted—Jake and his cock.

I clung to him, moving with him, gladly surrendering every inch of my cunt to him. "Oh, Jake. I'm yours. Take me."

"Damn right you are. You are always going to be mine. You are taken, Bree—forever. Deal with it."

I gasped and shuddered.

He fucked me so hard and deep, I felt as if I were drowning in waves of delicious, uninhibited delight. My world revolved around him. He was my world. My need and hunger for him threatened to consume me. I offered no resistance. I wanted to belong exclusively and eternally to him. My man. My Jake. My lover. My everything.

As he continued to shove into me, he buried his lips against my breasts and sucked hungrily. The intensity of joy dancing along the edge of my mind became too much to bear. I had to come and come hard.

I threw my head back and arched my breasts against his chest. I felt my pussy convulsing around his cock as I blew into tiny, happy pieces.

Moments later, he gripped my hips, fucked me wildly, roughly, almost brutally. He was hurting me as he attempted to brand me as his.

I clung to him, helpless to do anything but accept the pleasure-laced pain from the man I loved and needed with an insatiable hunger. Just as he bit into my breast, I gasped. He shuddered and then really slammed his cock as deep into me as he could get it. Firmly lodged in me, he shot his seed into my pussy. Or, as he had so rightly called it, his pussy. This was definitely his pussy and his alone.

Then we collapsed together, with his cock still inside me.

He kissed my lips and buried his face against my cheek.

Oh, hell, yeah. I held him close, thinking I could very easily get used to being fucked without protection and then having him hose down my pussy with his cum.

We slept in each other's arms. I woke first and went into the bathroom. I'd just stepped into the shower and started the water when I heard him relieving himself. Call me kinky or freaky or whatever, the sound turned me on. I closed my eyes and rubbed my pussy, thinking about his cock.

What I wouldn't give to have it back inside my greedy cunt. I sighed. Oh, well, I couldn't expect him to be ready for sex again for a while. So, imagine my delight, when moments later, I heard him turning on the sink. Then he opened the shower door and stepped inside with me.

I turned to face him. He was pumping his cock. He was aroused. I licked my lips in an effort to silently let him know I wanted him again.

Without a word, he turned me to face the tiles, spread my legs, and then I felt his cock at my entrance.

I licked my lips and my tilted my hips, but I had to tease him a little. "You know, it's customary for a man to ask permission before he plunges into a woman."

"Why should I have to ask permission for a pussy that belongs to me?"

He slapped my ass, making my cheeks sting. I loved it. And he knew it because he slapped both cheeks hard—several times until they stung.

Then he fondled my ass. "Now you're ready to be fucked. Got any objections?"

I wasn't born yesterday. I knew there was a time for talking and a time for fucking. I'm sure you knew which time it was for me. I braced myself against the tiles and pushed my hips back until I felt his cock head piercing my cunt. I stopped and closed my eyes, savoring the feeling. "Oh...my..."

"Are you complaining?"

"No...oh, no...Jake..."

He gripped my hips and pulled me back onto his cock.

As he slid slowly into me, the muscles of my belly rippled, and I moaned. "Oh, yes, Jake. I need you. Give it all to me. Every hard inch."

He bit my neck. "Take it. It's all yours, baby," he whispered and slipped balls deep inside me. "All yours, my lovely, sweet, delectable Bree."

I liked the idea that his cock belonged to me and he thought I was delectable. "Mine. All mine," I said with greedy delight and tightened my cunt muscles around him.

He groaned and thrust into me so hard, my breasts were smashed against the tiles. "Take it. Take it deep in your pussy. All of it."

I took it—every inch and it was absolutely incredible. We fucked hard and fast for several minutes. The only sounds in the bathroom being the running water, his grunts and my sighs each time he shot that big, sweet cock of his up into the regions of my pussy that loved cock best.

Then, when my inner thighs started trembling and I was close to coming, he pulled out of me.

"No." I protested.

Laughing softly, he turned me around to face him.

Any further protest died on my lips as he knelt in front of me.

After a brief glance up at me, he stuck out his tongue and slowly dragged it along the length of my wet slit.

"Ooooh."

He smiled up at me. "Do you like how my tongue feels on your pussy?"

"Oh, yes." I cupped my hands over my breasts and rotated my hips.

"Then you're going to love how it feels inside you." And he slipped his tongue between my slit and into me.

I gripped his head and pushed his face against my cunt. "Eat me, but do it slowly."

Holding my jiggling ass in his palms, he gave me the most delicious pussy suck, tongue fucking of my life. He licked and nibbled at my clit until I felt a powerful orgasm building. When he reached between my ass cheeks and pressed a finger into my ass, I couldn't bear anymore.

I sobbed with pleasure and came all over his face and tongue.

Unlike my former lovers, who removed their mouths after I'd come, Jake kept his lips, tongue, and fingers in motion, licking and thrusting right through my orgasm. His continued lovemaking, made my climax almost unbearably sweet.

While I was still enjoying the aftershocks of one of the most amazing releases, he rose, pressed me back against the tiles, and thrust his cock into me.

I gasped and clung to him.

He fucked me hard and roughly, almost punching his cock in and out of me until he came. When he had, he groaned my name and clutched my ass. He kept his cock buried deep in my pussy until he'd pumped the last drops of his cum deep inside me.

Only then did he ease his cock out of me. He wrapped his arms around me and held me close with his lips against my ear. "Bree. My Bree. My pussy and my woman."

He sounded like a happy, very satisfied man.

I nodded. "Your pussy and your woman-full of your cum." I lifted my face from his shoulder.

He pressed a long, slow, sweet kiss against my lips. When we came up for air, he cupped my face between his palms and stared down into my eyes. "Damn, woman, you are sweet."

I licked my lips and smiled. "You ain't so bad yourself, handsome."

"You do know that there's no going back, now? When I want you, I want you."

I licked my lips and stared silently up at him.

He stared back. "When I want to be held, I'll come to you. When I need a cheering section, I'll expect you to be there. And when I want pussy, I want pussy and no excuses about condoms or telling me we shouldn't do this again."

I nodded.

He caressed my cheek. "And when you need me, I'll be there for you."

I felt choked up with emotion. Even then I wasn't sure if I could trust his word. I just knew I was loving how things were playing out between us and I wanted him to mean what he was saying and promising.

"Bree? Okay?"

I nodded again.

He slapped my ass cheeks-hard. "That's my woman."

I gasped and ground my pussy against him.

"Stop that or I'll pin you against the wall and fuck you again," he warned.

I grabbed his cheek and pressed a finger against his ass.

He swore, eased me against the wall tile, and shoved his cock into me.

Clutching each other's asses and grunting like stuck pigs, we shared a rough, hard fuck. It only lasted a few minutes and he was jetting loads of cum into my pussy before I knew it. I didn't come, but strangely enough, I had no complaints as he eased his cock out of me.

I wrapped my arms around his neck and kissed him. "Thanks," I whispered.

"For what? I know you didn't come."

"Thanks for wanting me."

"I can't help wanting you. I can't help anything that's happened since the moment I laid eyes on you. All I know is that I want you as I've never wanted any other woman and I have to have you."

"You do have me."

"Thank God."

He hugged me briefly and then we showered together. It took a long time because he kept stopping to caress and kiss my breasts and fondle and slap my ass.

The man couldn't seem to keep his hands off my big butt. I like that in a man-a lover. Nevertheless, by the time we got out of the shower, my cheeks stung and if I'd had lighter skin, they would probably have been a bright, rosy red from all that delicious slapping.

It was only when we went back into the bedroom that some of my uncertainty of the night before returned. He'd probably had enough pussy to quench his thirst and would be less likely to be inclined to overlook my physical shortcomings.

I looked up and found him staring at me, as if he were really seeing me for the first time. And maybe he was because he was finally looking at me when he wasn't horny.

I bit my lip. Afraid of what I'd see in his gaze, I looked away.

"Damn, Bree, you are so sexy."

I jerked my head up. The look in his eyes and the sound of his voice convinced me of his sincerity. My remaining fears about how he viewed my nude body vanished.

I gave him a relieved look. "I'm glad you think so."

"I do. You know I love your big, round ass, but damn...your breasts are huge."

"They sag."

"Do I look as if that bothers me?"

"No," I admitted. "But my stomach isn't—"

"Oh, for the love of God, Bree. Get a clue, will you? Do I look as if there's anything about you that turns me off?"

"No."

"Then what's your problem, woman?"

"I ain't got one." I smiled and finished dressing with confidence.

When I had, he cupped my ass and pulled me against him. He gazed down at me with a bemused look in his eyes. "Oh, damn, Bree, I need you."

I felt his cock and shook my head. "Oh, no, you don't. You've had all the pussy you're getting for awhile."

He frowned. "Why?"

"Why?" I blinked up at him. "I'll tell you why. I've just showered and dressed and my pussy is sore."

He ground his cock against me. "You'd better get used to having it sore. Now that I know how sweet it is, you're going to have a problem keeping my cock out of it."

Although pleased, I danced out of his arms. "No more pussy for you now. Deal with it."

Of course he retaliated by slapping my ass-hard. When I gasped, he slapped each cheek again- even harder. Despite myself, my pussy gushed and I sucked in a breath. Still, I resisted the urge to bare my pussy and shamelessly let him fuck me again.

"I think I'll let you take me out to eat."

"I'm not hungry—at least not for food."

"Well, I am, Jake."

"I'd rather stay here and fuck you again."

"Too bad. I'm hungry. I want to eat."

"You want to eat?" He was still naked. He hefted his cock in his hand. "I have something here you could eat."

I licked my lips. "I'll take you up on that...delicious offer...soon. Right now, I want to eat—food. Got it?"

He sighed, but nodded.

We spent the weekend together. We went dancing that night and then returned to my apartment to spend the night fucking like bunnies. At one point while I lay on my back with him between my legs, fucking me deep and hard, I reached around his body and forced a finger into his ass.

He groaned and exploded, coming so hard, I thought he would flood my pussy.

Afterwards, he collapsed on me, gasping as if he couldn't catch his breath. I held him until his breathing returned to normal. "You like having your ass touched?"

"No. I don't."

He rolled off me and onto his side, with his back to me.

I wasn't having any of that shit. I urged him onto his stomach and straddled his lower legs. Then I parted his beautiful ass cheeks and covered them with biting kisses.

He groaned. I wet a finger in my mouth and then pressed it against his puckered hole.

He tensed. "Don't."

I removed my finger. "I know you like it, Jake, so what's wrong?"

"Get off of me."

I took my good time obeying him.

When I moved, he turned his back to me again.

So I slapped his ass.

He turned to face me. "What do you think you're doing?"

"Whatever I want."

His silence told me my reply had been unexpected.

Deciding I'd teased him enough, I pressed myself into his arms. "Hold me."

He held me, with his lips pressed against my forehead. I think that was his way of saying he'd overreacted to my touching that tight ass of his.

"Just so you know, Jake, I'll finger your ass whenever I like."

Although he stiffened against me, he didn't release me.

I took that as his acknowledgement that his ass was mine to touch as much as I liked. Nice, huh?

After breakfast on Sunday, we went for a long drive. When we got back, there were a dozen roses waiting in the lobby of my apartment building.

He carried them up to my apartment. "Hmmm. I wonder who your secret admirer is."

"You...you didn't send them?"

He arched a brow.

I panicked. This would be a very inconvenient time for Darren to send me roses. Darren. Oh, hell. I'd have to call him and tell him things had changed before he spent money on a plane ticket.

"Shall I read the card?" he asked when I remained silent.

"No." I snatched it from him and slipped it into my shoulder bag.

He laughed and bent to kiss the side of my neck. "Relax, Bree. They're from me."

I blushed and grimaced at him. "Cute, Jake. Real cute."

He slapped my ass-hard. "I'm glad you think so, darling."

Darling? Oh, man. If he kept this up I was going to lose my head over him. If he was only in this for a quick fuck or two, my heart would be in danger.

Inside my apartment, he undressed us both and then led me into the bedroom. When he moved to lie on top of me, I shook my head and pushed him onto his back. I then parted his legs and fondled his cock. "This looks good enough to eat."

"So eat it," he invited.

So I sucked that big, hard cock between my lips and played with his balls until he gripped the back of my head and started wildly fucking my face. I fought off the urge to gag...or at least I tried. I was relieved when he loosened his grip on the back of my head and I could withdraw part of his cock from my mouth as he came.

I tried to swallow it all but he took pity on me and slipped out of my mouth. Relieved, I finished him off with my hand. His cum slashed onto my breasts.

I stretched out on top of him. Since he was still semi-hard, I lifted my hips, gripped his cock, and sat down on it, driving it up into my pussy.

I smiled. "Nice."

"Nice?" He frowned. "I'll show you nice."

"Please do," I said.

He gave me a quick, hard fuck. I came within minutes. We fell asleep soon afterwards.

Later, we had dinner out. He spent the night, but we didn't make love. He held me until I fell asleep. After all, the love making during the weekend, I was exhausted. And I loved falling asleep with his arm tossed over my waist.

When I woke on Monday morning, he was gone. I was disappointed, but not worried. Not after the weekend, we'd spent together. I took a quick shower, ate breakfast, and headed to work.

The day was looking up until I encountered Lea in the company dining room.

She gave me a cold look and sat down across from me. "We need to talk."

I shook my head. "Unless its work related, there's nothing to talk about. And if it is work related, I don't want to talk work on my lunch hour."

"It's about Jake. I want you to leave him alone."

"Funny, that's the same thing I want you to do-leave him alone. You're married to his brother. Isn't that enough? How can you possibly think you can have them both?"

She compressed her lips. "I'm warning you, Bree, leave him the fuck alone. He's mine."

I leaned across the table and glared at her. "Yours? Maybe he used to be yours, but not anymore. Now he's mine and hell will freeze over before I allow you to get your cheating hands on him again."

"Whatever was between you two is over. He's mine now and I'm keeping him. Learn to deal with it or risk getting your ass kicked from here into next week."

"Are you...threatening me?"

"What do you think?"

"I think you don't want to fuck with me, Bree."

I laughed. "If you don't want me to kick your flat ass all over this room, I suggest you get the fuck out of my face—right now."

She sucked in an angry breath. "You haven't heard the last of this, you ungrateful bitch. And some men prefer a woman with a lot less ass than you're dragging around behind you."

That taunt might have stung at one time. "Well, since I've spent most of the weekend in Jake's arms, he's clearly not one of those men."

She lifted her right hand.

I was hard pressed not to reach across the table and slap her right into next week. I smiled instead—confident I had what she wanted but would never have again—Jake. "I wouldn't try that if I were you. If you dare call me a bitch again, I'll show you the meaning of the word. Now get the fuck out of my face. I'd call you a bitch, but that would be too kind."

Her lips trembled with rage and she turned and stalked away.

I stared after her, knowing I'd made an enemy and I'd need to watch her very closely.

Jake

I felt like I was on cloud nine on Monday. I spent the morning trying to work, but all I could think of was Bree. I resisted the urge to send roses to her office and called her instead. "I need to work late tonight, but can we have dinner on Tuesday?"

"I'd like that."

Her voice sounded soft and warm. I smiled. "Great. I'll see you around six on Tuesday?"

"Six will be fine."

"Great."

Chapter Twelve

Jake

The next three weeks slid by in a happy blur. Bree and I saw each other at least four times a week. On the days we didn't see each other, we talked at least twice. I no longer thought of Lea. Bree had all my time, attention, and sexual interest.

Each time I saw her, I became more and more enthralled with her. I liked everything about her. She was sweet, sexy, considerate, funny, and all mine. For the first time in my life, I felt completely satisfied with one woman. I never felt the urge to look at or date other women. I felt happy and content. I think she felt that way too. Everything between us was perfect.

We were sexually compatible, enjoyed similar hobbies, and when she told me about her ex-Darren and that she'd called him and told him about us, I knew then she was the woman for me. Just the way she said us put a big, silly grin on my face.

That night, after she fell asleep in my arms, I slipped out of her bed and called Mom to tell her I wanted her to meet Bree. To my surprise, she cried.

"I thought you'd be happy for me, Mom."

"I'm thrilled for you, Jake. I was so worried about you and Eddy."

"Why should you be worried about him? He's happily married."

"He is, but is she?"

I tensed, wondering how much she knew or suspected about my past with Lea. "What do you mean?"

"I'm no fool, Jake. I know what's been going on between the two of you."

Oh, hell.

"I know what she's been trying to do."

"You...do?"

"Yes. I know she's been coming between you and Eddy. She wants you both, Jake. I've always known and feared that."

I felt the back of my neck burning. "Mom, there's no danger of her and I...that's over."

"But at what cost?"

"What do you mean?"

She was silent for several moments before she responded. "Did you betray your brother, Jake?"

I closed my eyes. I wanted to lie, but I couldn't. Besides, it was time to get everything out in the open. "I came close, but...in spirit...yes, but I didn't actually...Mom, I—"

"And I have your word it's over between you and her?"

"Yes. It's been over since I met Bree."

"Then bring your Bree to see me. I'll be very happy to meet the woman who makes you happy."

After I hung up with Mom, I got back into bed with Bree.

She murmured my name and turned into my arms.

I kissed her lips, held her close, and drifted to sleep.

In the morning, I asked her to have dinner with me on Saturday.

"Where are we going? Any place fancy?" She smiled at me, her dark eyes warm. "Will I have to go shopping for a new outfit?"

"I doubt it. We're not going any place fancy. I'm just taking you to meet my mother."

She paused with a spoonful of cereal halfway to her lips. "Your mother? You want me to meet your mother?"

I nodded. "Yes."

"But...I'd love to meet your mother...if you're sure."

I reached across the table and took her hand in mine. "I'm very sure."

"It's not every day a man asks a woman to meet his mother."

I smiled.

She cast her gaze downward and played with her cereal. "There are certain...implications attached to introducing a woman to your mother, Jake."

I shrugged. "So I've heard."

"Jake." She lifted her gaze and stared at me.

I nodded. "I know what the implications are."

"But it's only been five weeks since we met and—"

"You're my woman and I want you to meet my mother. What's so hard to understand about that?"

She smiled and shook her head. "Nothing. Okay. It's a date."

"Great."

"Yeah. Great."

But she looked apprehensive.

"Don't worry, Bree, Mom is going to love you."

"I hope so." She bit her lip. "Did you tell her about me?"

"Yes. Why else would she want to meet you?"

"No. I mean...what did you tell her about me?"

"I told her all she needs to know to welcome you—I'm happy with you."

She gave me a brief, sweet smile. "Are you sure she won't be expecting a Lea look alike?"

"Trust me. That's the last thing she'd want."

"Doesn't she like Lea?"

"What is there about that bitch to like?"

"You liked her once."

"I never liked her. I was in lust with her. You? I like you—a lot and so will my mother."

"Oh, Jake, I hope so."

Saturday morning while I was having coffee, Jess called. Bree had taken work home with her so I'd spent the night in my own apartment. The moment I heard Jess's voice, I knew something was wrong. Her voice was low and nasal, as if she'd been crying. "Jess? What's wrong?"

"It's Malik, Jake."

Of course it was that dumb ass bastard. It was always him. "What about him?"

"He's left me."

Actually, I thought she was better off without his dumb ass, but I could hardly tell her that. "Oh, damn, honey. I'm so sorry. Is there anything I can do?"

"I could use a shoulder to cry on, Jake."

"Sure. When?"

"Now."

"Now?"

"Yes. Unless you have plans."

I was supposed to pick Bree up in two hours so we could go shopping for a dress for our dinner with mom that night. But I was sure Bree didn't need my help buying a dress. I knew I'd like her in anything she chose. "No. Just give me forty minutes and I'll come over."

"Thanks."

"There's no thanks necessary. I'll see you soon."

"Hurry."

After hanging up with Jess, I called Bree. I'd mentioned Jess to her so she knew about her. She listened in silence while I told her about that dumb ass Malik leaving Jess an emotional wreck.

"So can you manage shopping alone?"

"Sure." She sounded disappointed, but understanding. "Of course you have to be there for her. I can meet your mom another time."

"Oh, no. We're still on for tonight. I'll just need a few hours to make sure she's all right. Go shopping and I'll call you later."

"Are you sure?"

"Yes."

"I'll go shopping, but I think we should reschedule with your Mom. I don't want you to feel like you have to rush away from a friend in need."

"Are you sure?"

"Yes. If it's not too late when you get home, call me."

When I contrasted her reaction to how Lea would have ranted and raved, I was doubly thankful that I now had a woman in my life I could respect. Respect? What was the point in denying it to myself? I was in love with Bree. As soon as I got the situation with Jess under control, I was going to find out if she was in love with me. If she wasn't, she sure as hell would be before I was finished with her.

"I will, honey. I'll talk to you later."

"Okay."

I called Mom and then I drove to Jess's place.

Her reaction to canceling our dinner plans surprised me. "Are you sure it's wise to cancel a date with Bree to be with Jess?"

"Wise? I told Bree and she doesn't have a problem with it."

"Are you sure about that, Jake?"

"Of course I'm sure. She knows Jess and I are just friends."

She sighed. "Okay, but please make sure you go see her as soon as you leave Jess's house."

"I will and I'll call you to reschedule dinner."

"Okay, dear."

On the way over to Jess's place, I stopped by a florist. I ordered a dozen roses sent to Bree and bought a single red one for Jess, hoping it would help cheer her up.

Of course if I'd known the mischief Lea was up to, not only would I not have gotten the rose, I would have taken Bree with me when I went to see Jess. But I didn't know so I drove to Jess's house with no thought of the mess and heartache that would begin for me the moment Jess opened her front door-stark naked.

I stared at her in stunned surprise. I hadn't seen her nude since we were lovers years earlier. Over the years, I'd been aware of how beautiful and sexy she was, but in a generic way. She was married and a good friend. I didn't spend any time ogling her or thinking about how good she looked naked.

Now I couldn't believe she was standing there without a stitch of clothing on. "Jess. What' going on? You're naked."

"I'm glad someone's noticed I'm still an attractive woman."

She was, but I hadn't said anything about that and I didn't intend to. But she didn't seem to need much encouragement. She leaned into me and wrapped her arms around my neck. I could feel her large, firm breasts pressed against my chest. She reached down and cupped her hand around my cock.

I swore softly, stiffened, and jerked away. "Jess. What the hell do you think you're doing?"

She lifted her face to mine. I saw the tears in her dark eyes and smelled the alcohol on her breath. She was drunk and hurt.

"Jake. Oh, Jake, he left me for another woman. It hurts like hell. Please, Jake. I need to be held."

"Fine. I'll hold you—after you put some clothes on."

"Now, Jake. I'm hurting now. And I need to be held now."

Oh, damn. Later, I kept wishing I'd insisted she dressed first. But with her standing there in tears telling me she needed a hug, what could I do? How could I say no to her? And what did it matter if she were naked? It wasn't as if I were going to touch her.

When she put her arm around my neck again, I embraced her, brushing my lips against her cheek. "It's all right, honey. You'll be all right, but we need to get some clothes on you."

She collapsed against me and I lifted her into my arms, carried her inside, and closed the door with my foot. And one of the longest days of my life began. I spent the next few hours peeling her naked body out of my arms and doing my best to keep her from grabbing my cock every time I let my guard down for even a moment. Each time she managed to wrap her fingers around my cock, she'd tell me she needed a fuck.

"If I weren't involved with Bree, I would fuck you, but I can't, Jess."

"Why not? I won't ever tell anyone and I just need one fuck. It's been months since Malik made love to me and I'm hurting, Jake. Please. Just this once-for the sake of our friendship."

Though I tried to be understanding, I was annoyed and angry that she'd think I would endanger my relationship with Bree for anyone-her included. "No. You know I love you, Jess. And you know I'd do anything to help, if I could, but I will not fuck you. I'm involved..." I shook my head and met her dark gaze. "I'm in love with Bree and even if she never found out, I'd know I'd been unfaithful. I'll spend as much time with you as you need, but I am not going to fuck you. Is that clear?"

Apparently it wasn't because she responded by reaching for my cock again. That's when I'd had enough. I grabbed her hand and pulled her through the house to the master bathroom. I filled the tub with cold water and picked her up.

She linked her arms around my neck and gave me a drunken smile. "Finally."

I almost felt bad about pushing her into the cold water and holding her there. She gasped and tried to get away but I'd had enough of fighting her off. She was going to have to learn the hard way to keep her hands off Bree's goods.

When I finally let her up, she was shaking and crying softly. Steeling myself against her tears and hurt silence, I wrapped a towel around her body. "Dry off and dress. While you do I'll make some coffee and find you something to eat."

"I hate you," she whispered.

I caressed her cheek. "I hate you too, honey."

I left her in the bathroom with tears streaming down her face. Half an hour later when I'd made coffee and an omelet with fried onions and chunks of cheese, ham, and bacon, and toast, she stumbled into the kitchen fully dressed.

She kept her gaze turned downward and I realized she was now sober and embarrassed. "I'm sorry, Jake," she muttered.

"Oh, honey, it's all right." I walked over to her and engulfed her in a warm embrace, kissing her cheek.

She sobbed and clung to me. This time there was no attempt to press her breasts against my chest. This embrace was one shared by two friends. Jess, the drunken, seductress was gone. Thank God.

We sat at her table and I encouraged her to eat as she told me how she'd come home early the previous day and found a strange woman spread eagle on the bed in one of the guest rooms. Her wrists had been handcuffed to the headboard and her ankles bound to the bottom of the bedrail.

And that stupid ass Malik had been fucking the hell out of her.

When Jess screamed at him, he'd jumped off the bed. His cock was covered with blood and that's when she realized he was fucking her without protection while she was having her period. The towels he'd put under her ass were soaked with blood.

As I listened, I wished I'd knocked him on his ass the one time we had argued. Cheating on her was bad enough but to do it in the house they shared and with a female who barely looked old enough to be legal, was like rubbing salt into her wounds. God only knew why but she seemed to love the bastard and I knew his infidelity hurt her.

I reached for her hand and squeezed it. "I know it hurts, believe me, I know how someone you love cheating can hurt." I paused and frowned. Actually I didn't know. I'd been in big time lust with Lea, but I now knew I had not been in love with her.

Still, at the time of her dumping me for Ed, it had hurt like hell. "I got over it-over Lea and you'll get over him."

Tears swelled in her eyes. "But I don't want to get over him. I want him back."

She wanted him back after what she'd walked in on him doing? Shit. This was going to take awhile. "I know that feeling too. But when you meet the right man, you won't want him back."

"What makes you think Malik wasn't the right man?"

Oh, hell, how could a woman as intelligent as Jess be so damned blind when it came to the no good man in her life? I shrugged. "Because he cheated on you?"

"It was a mistake. Haven't you ever made one?"

Oh, damn, this was going to be a long night. "I've made plenty."

"Then don't act as if you haven't."

Great. Just great. I gave up time with Bree for this. "Fine."

"I'm being such a bitch to you. I'm sorry. Please don't go."

If she expected me to disagree with her, she could forget it. She was being bitchy, but then what good were friends you couldn't be an occasional bitch with?

"I'm not going anywhere, Jess."

She gulped in a breath and then sobbed. "It hurts like hell, Jake."

I nodded. "I know, honey. I know."

She pushed her plate away, tears streaming down her cheeks. She held out a hand to me, her lips trembling.

Chapter Thirteen

Jake

I made her a cup of decaf tea, poured a healthy dose of brandy in it, took her hand in mine, and took her to bed. I held her until she fell asleep, then I slipped out of bed, left the bedroom, and called Bree.

She answered on the first ring. "Jake? Are you on your way?"

She sounded anxious and I felt guilty that I'd taken so long to call her.

"Hi, honey. I just got Jess settled down to sleep."

"Great."

"Not so great."

"Oh. How is she?"

I hesitated. I wanted to be completely honest with her, but I didn't want to put Jess in a bad light. Bree's and my relationship was still new and I didn't want to risk her misunderstanding if I told her the whole truth. So I didn't. That was mistake number two or three. My first mistake was underestimating how much trouble a vengeful and jealous bitch like Lea could cause.

"She's in bad shape, Bree. She's asleep, but I doubt she'll sleep through the night."

"No?"

"No. So I'd like to stick around here for a while...maybe spend the night in case she wakes up crying. Is that all right with you?"

"You...you...you want to spend the night with her?"

If I hadn't been so damned tired from fighting Jess off for hours, I might have picked up on the hint in the question. But I didn't. "Yes—in her guestroom...unless you have a problem with it."

"In the guestroom?"

"Yes."

"Ah...no. No. Of course not. You're good friends and she needs you. Of course you have to stay with her. When will I see you?"

"I'll call you tomorrow."

"Ah...okay. Good night."

I hesitated. I wanted to tell her that I loved her, but I was vain enough to want to be able to watch the look in her eyes the first time I told her I loved her. And that was yet another mistake. If I had told her then how I really felt, she might not have been so willing to put the worst spin on things with Jess later.

"Good night, sweetheart."

I knew I'd made the right decision to stay-at least for Jess, when the sounds of her muffled sobs woke me in the middle of the night. I'd left both bedroom doors open for just such an occasion. I slipped out of the bed in the guest room and ran down the hall to her bedroom.

She looked surprised when I turned the light on. "Jake." She sat up in bed, her arms open. "I thought you were gone."

"Oh, no, honey. I'm here for you." I climbed into bed with her and hugged her. I held her until she fell back to sleep, then I went back to the guest room.

In the morning, she was tear free, but I could almost feel her pain. I knew I couldn't leave her. While she was soaking in the tub, I went into the living room and called Bree.

"Hi, Jake. I was just thinking about you. Where are you?"

"I'm still with Jess."

"Oh."

That one word held a wealth of disappointment. "Is something wrong?"

"No. I just need to talk to you. There's something I need to tell you...something important."

"I'm listening, Bree."

"It's not something I want to tell you over the phone. I need to tell you in person."

"Okay. Ah...is it something good?"

"I'm not sure how you're going to feel about it, but I don't want to discuss it on the phone. How is she today?"

"She's not crying anymore, but frankly Bree, I'm worried about her. He's a dumb ass bastard, but she loves him so much. She's hurt and afraid and I'd just like to spend another day with her-but only if you're okay with it. If you need to talk to me now, I'll be there in half an hour."

She sighed. "Ah...no. It can wait."

"Are you sure?"

"Yes. Tomorrow is fine. I'll see you then."

"Yes. I'm sure she'll be better able to cope by then. I'll call you later and maybe we can—"

"It's okay. Stay with her and give her the moral support she needs. I'll see you some time tomorrow."

"Okay. Bree?"

"Yes, Jake?"

"I...I..." I moistened my lips. "I can't wait to see you tomorrow."

"Me too."

"There's something I need to discuss with you too."

"Something good?" She asked.

"I hope you'll think it is."

"I'll see you tomorrow, Jake."

And that was yet another mistake in my endless list of mistakes. I should have left Jess and gone to Bree. I was trying to be there for Jess as she'd been there for me when Lea dumped me. Still if I'd known how much I was risking, I would have left-with Jess's blessings. But I didn't know. So I stayed. I was a little uneasy and eager to see Bree and tell her how I felt and learn what she wanted to tell me, but I was confident that things would work out fine when I saw her the next night. The only problem with that plan was Lea saw her that night.

Bree

After I hung up the phone with Jake, I felt tears prick my eyes. I told myself I was being a jealous, selfish bitch, but I wanted Jake with me. How many nights did he need to spend with his friend?

I ran a hand over my belly and gave an angry shake of my head. He had to stay with her for as long as she needed him. Yes, I wanted him with me. Yes, I was ready to admit I loved him, but that didn't mean I had to start being mean-spirited and overly needy. Men didn't like needy women.

I spent the rest of the day pampering myself. I had breakfast delivered from my favorite, expensive restaurant, ate it in bed, and then spent an hour dozing in the tub. Then, feeling tired and more than a little ashamed of my selfish desire to call Jake and insist he come home-to me, I went to bed. I lay awake for nearly an hour, wishing Jake's hard, nude body was curled behind mine before I fell asleep.

The phone woke me several hours later. Thinking it might be Jake, I shot up in bed and grabbed the cordless phone off the nightstand. "Hello? Jake?"

"Hardly. This is Lea. I'm in your lobby. We need to talk."

"We have nothing to say to each other."

"Yes, we do. If you want to know what's really going on between Jake and his *friend* Jess, let me in."

"I know what's going on. She's upset and he's—"

"He's there fucking the hell out of her."

I sucked in an angry breath. "You lying, scheming bitch. You'll do anything to break us up, won't you? Well, it won't work. I don't believe you."

"I thought you wouldn't."

"Then why are you calling trying to make trouble between us?"

"I have proof of what he's really doing with her. If you want to keep your head buried in the sand like an ostrich, fine. Don't let me in. You'll learn he can't be trusted the hard way—just as I did. If you want to know the truth about him before it's too late, buzz me in."

Looking back, I realized if I hadn't been so emotional because of my condition and if I'd had any inkling of how Jake felt about me, I wouldn't have been tempted to listen to her. I knew her motives were suspect and she couldn't be trusted. Actually, I knew she was jealous of my relationship with Jake and wanted to break us up. I should have remembered that.

But my hormones were out of whack. I was jealous, insecure, and foolish enough to give her the foothold she needed. I buzzed her in. Ten minutes later, she told me she was pregnant. Of course I could see that the moment she walked in the door. She's very slender...almost skinny and the bulge in her belly was unmistakable.

I shrugged. "Congrats to you and Ed."

She shook her head. "It's not his baby."

I shook my head and clenched my right hand into a fist to keep from slapping her so hard her head would spin around on that skinny neck of hers. I knew what she was implying and I didn't want to hear it. "Just stop right there. If you're going to try to tell me it's Jake's baby, let me save you the trouble and tell you I don't believe you."

She tossed her head angrily. "Why not?"

"Because he told me he hasn't touched you since before you dumped him for his brother."

"And you believe him?"

"Yes. I do."

"Why?"

"Because he's spent the last few weeks with me. I know he's not interested in you or anyone else."

She shook her head. "Oh, God does he have you snowed...just as he did me. I thought he was faithful...that he loved me until I caught him cheating. That's when I turned to Ed on the rebound."

I stared at her. "Do you actually expect me to believe he cheated on you instead of you dumping him when his brother won the lottery?"

"Yes, I do because it's true."

"Sure it is. And the sky is falling too. Isn't it?"

"Like you, I trusted him. I was so in love with him that I was unfaithful with him. His brother is worth two of him any day of the week. Even now, I love him." She rubbed her belly. "And I just wanted to save you the grief I had with him."

"What makes you think I believe any of what you're saying?"

"Look. I know I've been a bit of a bitch, but you don't know what he's done to me. He's made me this way. You can't trust him, Bree. I have proof of that. He's playing and using us both."

I shook my head and without thinking, I rubbed my belly.

Her gaze narrowed and she stared at me. "Oh, God, he's got you pregnant too. Why didn't you make the bastard use a condom?"

I snatched my hand away from my stomach. "I didn't say I was pregnant."

"But you are. Aren't you? I know from experience how he refuses to use a condom. You let him fuck you once without one when you think it's safe, the next thing you know he's refusing to fuck you unless you let him do it bareback. I know how it goes with him."

I think that's when the tide of my disbelief started to turn. Isn't that what had happened between us the first time we made love? He'd threatened to leave and not come back if I made him use a condom. I shook my head, but the seed of doubt she'd planted started to take root.

"Oh, Bree, come on and wake up."

I shook my head again, fighting back tears. I wasn't ready to believe the worst of him not without proof…which she whipped out.

"Fine. You think he's just comforting his Jess? Think again. They're lovers. How do I know? I'll tell you. He's gotten me so crazy with jealousy that I followed him and I have proof."

"Proof? What proof? If you think I'm going to consider your word proof, you'd better think again."

"Like you, I trusted him—until his cheating drove me into Ed's arms. Now he's back with that damn Jess again. Here they are in living color." She opened her purse and extended several pictures.

I stared at her, but made no move to take the pictures. Still, my heart was racing and I was afraid of the tendrils of belief in her words that was starting to eat at me. "What's that?"

"Proof that he and Jess are lovers. He's over there now, probably fucking her without a condom-just as he did with you and me. Hell, in a couple of months, she'll probably be pregnant with his baby too. Take them. See how she greeted him and then tell me you don't believe they're lovers."

I swallowed hard and shook my head. But I was so afraid of what the pictures might reveal.

"What's the matter, Bree? Can't face the truth?"

That did it. I snatched the pictures from her and quickly wished I hadn't. The first one showed Jake facing a very naked, beautiful, voluptuous black woman. The next picture showed her with her arms around his neck, leaning into him with her big, perfect, firm breasts pressed against his chest. Damn the hussy, she was shapely with long legs and not an ounce of excess fat on her.

"Notice that single red rose he gave her. Do you know what that means? He's pledging his love and devotion to her while he has both of us pregnant with his baby. Damn him and damn her for taking him from us."

I swallowed hard and tried to blink back the tears stinging my eyes. The next picture pushed me over the edge of disbelief far down into the valley of painful belief. That picture showed Jake cradling the naked woman in his arms. The final picture showed her with her hand between his legs.

Lea opened her purse. "There's more...of them in her bedroom together and taking a bath together after they finished fucking. Do you want to see them?"

I shook my head and felt a tear stream down my cheek. I pushed the pictures at her and turned away, pressing my hand against my mouth.

"I know it hurts and I'm sorry I had to hurt you, but I thought you had a right to know."

I wrapped my arms around my body and closed my eyes. When I heard my apartment door open and close, I sobbed and sank down to the floor. *Jake. Jake, how could you?*

I don't know how long I lay there before I got to my feet and went into my bedroom. I lay on my side and cried myself to sleep. I woke in the middle of the night knowing I couldn't face Jake again-not until I had a handle on my feelings.

I went online for an hour and then I got on the phone. Ten hours later, I was on a plane to California and Darren.

Chapter Fourteen

Jake

On Monday morning, I woke to the smell of coffee and home fries filling the air. I got out of bed, took care of my needs in the bathroom, and then made my way to the kitchen.

Jess, dressed in the sleek, dark suits she wore to work and fully made up, turned to smile at me from the range. "Hey."

There was a hint of sadness in her gaze, but I also saw resolve there. I walked across the kitchen and kissed her cheek. "Hey yourself. How are you?"

She sighed, then smiled, and nodded. "Hopeful. It still hurts like hell, but I'm going to be okay."

"You are?"

She nodded. "Yes." She linked an arm around my neck and kissed my chin. "Thanks so much."

I hugged her close. "Of course."

She sighed again and then pushed me away. "Sit down, eat your breakfast, and then go call your Bree and thank her for her kindness in lending you to me for the weekend. Tell her I owe her a big one...as I do you."

I shook my head. "You may owe her, but you don't owe me squat. You don't have a thing I want or need—except your continued friendship."

Her eyes welled with tears, but she smiled. "You've got that for life, buster."

"Same here."

"Fine. Eat up and then go see your Bee."

"And you're going to be okay?"

"Oh yeah. I'm not going to give Malik the satisfaction of hurting me any longer."

"You mean you don't want him back after all?'

She hesitated, then shook her head. "No. He wants a jailbait lover, fine. They can have each other. It's time for me to move on."

I nodded and smiled. "That's my Jess. You're a beautiful, sexy woman that any man with half a brain would love a chance to fall in love with."

She nodded and smiled. "Damn right." Her smile vanished and she sighed. "I'm so sorry for how I behaved when you arrived, Jake. I was drunk and out of my head."

I grimaced. "We're good friends. So you met me at the door naked and tossed yourself into my arms and begged me to fuck you at least once." I shrugged and grinned at her. "So what?"

She laughed. "Was it that bad?"

"Yes, but that's what friends are for, Jess. So let's not hear anymore about it. Okay? It's over and done with. Yes?"

She nodded. "Okay."

After I ate, I grabbed my cell phone and called Bree on my way to the guest bathroom to shower. I got her answering machine. I left a brief message. "Hi, sweetheart, it's Jake. I'm eager to see you. Can you make lunch today? I can do it anytime you like. I'll call you at your office around ten. Bye, honey."

I didn't realize anything was wrong until I called her office from work and learned she wasn't in. That surprised me. "She took the day off?"

"She's on vacation."

I blinked. "What? For how long?"

"Two weeks."

Two weeks? She and I had started to discuss the possibility of taking a joint vacation. Why the hell would she have taken vacation without talking to me first? "Thank you." I hung up and called her apartment. I got her answering machine again. I left another message, asking her to call me so we could have lunch. When I hadn't heard from her by twelve-thirty, I took an extended lunch, got in my car, and drove to her apartment.

The first thing I noticed was that her car was not in her parking space. I called her apartment and hung up when I got her answering machine. She wasn't at work and she wasn't home. So where the hell was she? And why the hell hadn't she told me she was going on vacation for two damned weeks?

I spent the rest of the day waiting to hear from her and checking my cell for non-existent messages. It wasn't until I got home that I realized I hadn't checked my answering machine on my landline. There were several messages.

I sank down on the sofa and listened to them.

"Jake, this is Gabrielle."

Gabrielle? Oh, damn. She never called herself that with me. I braced myself.

"By now you've probably noticed I'm not around-that is if you've managed to tear yourself away from your *friend*, Jess. I don't know why you felt the need to lie to me, but thanks to Lea, once I knew you had, I knew what I had to do. Of course it's over between us, but as you have Jess to fuck, I doubt you'll even notice I'm gone, but I'm fairly certain Darren will be happy to see me...even if you aren't."

I felt as if someone had strapped a tight band across my chest. I felt as if it was constricting my breathing. The blood rushed to my head and a rage I'd never felt before surrounded and consumed me.

"Lea, you bitch. What have you done?" I shot to my feet, felt dizzy, and fell back against my chair, holding my head and gasping to get air into my lungs. When I had my breathing back under control, I stormed out of the apartment, got in my car, and drove over to Ed and Lea's place.

I pounded on the door.

Ed opened the door. His face contorted when he saw me. "You bastard. How dare you come here?"

"Where the hell is that bitch you call a wife?" I demanded.

"You can say that after what you've done to her?"

I narrowed my gaze. "I haven't done anything to her yet, but I intend to."

"The hell you will." He threw a punch at me.

I blocked it and giving into my anger, I knocked him on his ass. Then I reached down and snatched him up from the floor by his collar. I balled my hand into a fist and drew it back to hit him.

"No, Jake. Don't you dare hit him again."

At the sound of mom's voice, I released my hold on Ed's shirt. His knees buckled, but he managed to stay on his feet. I turned and found mom standing several feet from us with her arm around Lea's shoulders. The jealous bitch had crocs streaming down her cheeks.

"Oh, Jake, haven't you done enough to us?" She wailed, and I do mean wailed. The people in the next block probably heard her.

The bitch had somehow turned Bree against me, had no doubt lied to Ed, and my mom, and now she was trying to make herself look like some damned victim. Judging by the way Mom and Ed were looking at me, she'd succeeded.

At that moment, when I was certain I'd lost Bree forever, just when I realized how much I loved her, I could have easily wrung Lea's neck, and happily gone to jail for it. Instead, I glared at her, looked at Mom, and turned and walked away.

I heard Mom calling to me, but I shook my head and kept walking. If I went back there, there would be no force on earth strong enough to keep me from wrapping my hands around Lea's neck and strangling the bitch to within an inch of her miserable, cheating life.

I spent a long, angry night tossing in my sleep, wondering where Bree was and what Lea had told her. I'd never needed to talk to anyone so much before. Chuck was on vacation and Jess was too emotionally fragile for me to dump on.

I felt so alone and so damned scared every time I thought of Bree. For the first time in my life, I was in love and Lea had ruined my chances of happily ever after-just because she was a jealous, greedy bitch who wanted it all-my cock and Ed's money.

I guess I fell asleep somewhere near dawn. I don't know how long I slept before I felt a soft hand on my cheek. I snapped open my eyes to find my mother sitting on the side of my bed staring down at me. "Mom?"

She nodded. "Yes, Jake. I've come to hear your side of the story."

All the anger, fear, and pain of the last day crashed over me and the next thing I knew, I was lying with my face against her body, bawling like a baby.

She cried with me with and rocked me in her arms, telling she loved me-no matter what. I fell asleep in her arms. When I woke again, she told me she'd called in sick for me. Over coffee, I told her about Bree's message.

That's when Mom told me, Lea had told her and Ed she was pregnant with my child-as a result of rape. Mom shook her head. "I knew you had not raped her and I told her and Ed so. Then she said it hadn't actually been rape, but that it was your child."

"It's not mine." I paused. Oh, God, at least I hoped it wasn't. I hadn't come in her, but I had been inside her when I'd been very horny and aroused at the time.

She nodded, her eyes filling with tears. "I knew it couldn't be. I know you and Ed have had problems since you met her, but I knew you wouldn't...couldn't betray him in such a vile manner."

I compounded by mistake with Bree by remaining silent. I couldn't admit to Mom that I had actually betrayed Ed. I swallowed hard and admitted the truth.

After staring at me with a shocked look on her face, Mom shook her head. "It was wrong of you, Jake, but I know she pursued you—even after she'd landed Ed."

"Yes, she did, but I shouldn't have succumbed to her."

"No, you shouldn't have, but I knew you hadn't raped her."

While I wasn't half as sure as she was, her confidence restored some of my self-confidence. "Thanks, Mom, but I think Ed believes her."

"Why should he? In his heart, he knows what she is, but he loves her so much and now that she's pregnant, what can he do but stand by her for the baby's sake?"

Poor bastard. He was in for a rough time with that bitch. God help the baby.

She sighed. "But right now we have to figure out how to make things right with your Bree."

I shook my head. "I don't know if that's possible. You know how good Lea is at what she does. She must have done a good job on Bree to make her believe there was something physical between Jess and me."

"Jess?" Mom smiled suddenly. "That's it."

"What's it?"

"Jess works for a security company. Surely she has connections and can find Bree for you so you can explain."

"Jess's in bad shape at the moment. If I ask her for help, I'll have to tell her why Bree left."

"Why would that be so wrong?"

"I don't want her having a guilt trip because of some lies Lea made up."

Mom glanced away briefly before meeting my gaze. "Are they lies, Jake?"

"Yes. They are. There's nothing physical between Jess and me."

"Lea said you broke up her marriage."

"I didn't break up Jess's marriage. Lea is a two-timing, backstabbing, lying bitch."

"Jake."

I sighed and shook my head. "I'm sorry about the language, Mom, but there's no other way to say it. There's nothing between Jess and I but friendship."

"Then how do you explain the pictures?"

"Pictures? What pictures?"

That's when she told me about the pictures of me and Jess at the door of her house. That's when I knew why Bree had gone from being supportive of my being there for Jess to believing I'd been sleeping with her. Lea must have shown her the pictures as well.

I sighed. "I'm sure the pictures look incriminating, Mom, but they are misleading. Here's what happened."

She shook her head. "If you say they're misleading, that's good enough for me, Jake."

"Thanks, but I want to tell you what really happened and why." When I had, I looked at her. "So you see why I couldn't possibly ask for Jess's help without making her feel guilty."

"She's your friend, Jake. She'd want to know that she played even an unwitting part in this and want to help make it right."

I shook my head. "No. She's too fragile right now. I can't risk placing any more stress on her just yet."

"But what if Bree is with this...her ex and she stays with him and you lose her? Jess wouldn't want that."

"It won't come to that."

"How do you know?"

"I...I don't know. I just know I can't risk dumping on Jess right now."

"Are you sure?"

"Yes."

Mom, being Mom and feeling as if she knew best, didn't listen to me. And looking back, I'm glad she didn't.

Bree

By the time my plane landed in L.A., I knew coming had been a mistake. As much as I was angry with Jake and as much as I hurt all over, I wasn't going to make things worse by trying to use Darren. He's never been anything but sweet, kind, and considerate to me. He didn't deserve to be a pawn between me and Jake.

Uttering a silent prayer of thanks that I hadn't actually called Darren, I found a hotel, and checked in. Three days later, as I returned to my room after lunch, I'd had time to get over my anger and calm down. I'd also had time to wonder if I'd been foolish for running away from Jake based on Lea's word. For all I knew she'd somehow faked those pictures. If they were real, how did I know when they were taken or who the woman was? I've never met Jess.

The woman in the pictures with Jake could very well have been another lover that he's told me about. Why hadn't I at least confronted him and given him a chance to explain? How did I know he didn't have a perfectly logical explanation?

I sank down into one of the chairs by the window and sighed. I'd been a fool. I touched my stomach. At the very least, for the sake of our baby, I needed to at least talk to him face to face.

I was going home and confronting him. I'd give him the benefit of the doubt and listen to what he had to say with an open mind. After that I'd decide if I should tell him I was pregnant.

I rose and walked over to the telephone. As I was about to pick it up to make reservations to go home, it rang. I wondered who it could be. Mom was the only one who knew where I was and I'd talked to her that morning.

Frowning, I answered it. "Hello?"

"Hi. Is this Gabrielle? Bree?"

"Yes. And you are?"

"Jessica Abbott."

"I'm sorry. Who are you?"

"Jake's friend, Jess."

"You." I clenched my free hand into a fist. "We have nothing to say to each other."

"We do if you've been listening to Lea's lies and I'm very afraid you have. I'm downstairs in the hotel lobby. Can I come up? I know you've seen some incriminating pictures of Jake and me, but…"

I closed my eyes and dropped onto the bed. "Then the pictures were real?"

"Not the way I'm sure Lea portrayed them. Look, Bree, as you must know, I know how painful infidelity can be. My husband…"

I understood her pain and hurt with her. "I know," I said softly when her voice trailed off.

She took a deep breath before she continued. "Even if I were so inclined, which I'm not, Jake only has eyes for you. Please let me come up to your room and explain those pictures."

I wanted to believe her and to believe that Jake hadn't cheated on me. I nodded. "Okay." I gave her my room number.

We faced each other fifteen minutes later. Just looking at her, I had to fight out a feeling of inadequacy. She was tall and shapely without an ounce of fat on her entire body. Worse, she was gorgeous. And she wanted me to believe that Jake preferred me to her? Apparently, Jake wanted me to believe it too. I wasn't sure why though or why he seemed to want me back.

"Did Jake send you?"

She shook her head. "No. In fact, he'd be very upset if he knew I was here. He didn't want me to know how his trying to be a friend to me broke you two up."

I thought of her with Jake and felt my temper rising. "What broke us up were those pictures of you naked with your hands where they had no business being."

She sighed and nodded. "You're right and all I can say is I'm so sorry." First Lea and now her going after Jake. I clenched my hand into a fist to help me resist the urge to slap her. "Why are you here?"

"Because he is one of my best friends and I am not going to be responsible for coming between him and you...not when I know how he feels about you."

If she knew how he felt about me, she knew more than I did. I wasn't sure I believed her, but since I'd already decided to go back and hear his side of the story, I might as well hear hers as well.

"I saw the pictures of you two together. You were naked and he —"

"I was naked, yes, but I was also drunker than I've been since college. And he had a difficult time holding me off without hurting my feelings. But he did because of how he feels about you."

"And just how is that?"

"Why don't you come back to Philly with me and find out first hand?"

"I'm going back, but not with you."

She sighed again and nodded. "I understand."

"Good. Now tell me why I shouldn't slap you into next week for putting your hands on him."

Chapter Fifteen

Jake

Bree had been gone a week and I felt close to losing my mind when I came home from work one day and saw her car in my second parking space. She wasn't in it so I raced up to my apartment.

When I opened the front door and rushed inside, she rose from the sofa and turned to face me.

I can't begin to tell you how I felt seeing her after what felt like a lifetime. I wanted to run across the room and engulf her in a bear hug, hold her tight, and never let her go. But I stood frozen to the spot, staring at her, my heart pounding with joy because she was there. My Bree, my love had come back to me. I knew I had a lot of explaining to do and there was a good chance she wouldn't believe me, but at least I'd have a chance to talk to her...hold her...just...hell, watch her sleep.

She spoke first. "Hi, Jake."

At the soft sound of her voice and the uncertain look in her eyes, I felt as if a wellspring of emotion burst inside me. This was my woman. My Bree and I was damned if I'd allow her to go another moment without knowing how I felt.

"Damn, Bree, I love you," I whispered.

When she gave me a wide-eyed, silent stare, I hurried across the room and swept her into my arms. I hugged her tightly, until she protested. Then I cupped her face...her beloved face between my palms, and pressed a long, slow kiss against her lips.

"I love you."

She moaned and wound her arms around my neck. She dragged her lips away from mine, and murmured something softly against my ear that sent a chill of fear and joy through me.

I pulled away from her and stared down into her dark gaze. "What? What did you say?"

She moistened her lips. "I said I love you too."

"No. Not that." I waved a hand impatiently. "I heard that. What else did you say?"

She chewed at her bottom lip. "Nothing much. I just said—"

"Bree."

She sighed and shrugged. "I said...I'm preg...we're going to have a baby. Is that what you wanted to hear again?"

"A baby." I raked both hands through my hair. "A baby? You're pregnant? We're having a baby?"

She nodded, her dark, anxious gaze trained on my face. "Yes. How do you feel about it?"

"How the hell do you think I feel about it?"

"I...I don't know."

"You don't?" I stared at her. "The woman I love is having my baby. How should I feel?"

"I don't know."

"Then I'll tell you. I'm happy...ecstatic...delighted."

"You are?"

I snatched her back into my arms and gave her a bear hug. "Yes. Oh, God, yes."

She tipped up her head and I kissed her and kissed her. Driven by my love and lust for her, I went wild, devouring her. When some semblance of reality returned, we were both naked on the loveseat. She faced me, straddling me with my cock buried as deep in her honey-hot, pregnant pussy as I could get it.

As she rocked her hips and fucked herself on my cock, I greedily sucked her big, beautiful breasts and caressed the belly where our baby grew. Next I reached around her body and thrust a finger up into her lovely, dark asshole.

She moaned, her tight pussy convulsed, and I felt her coming all over my cock. I withdrew my finger, shoved my cock as hard and deep into her as I could and exploded. As I shot my cum up into her pussy, I felt as if I'd died and gone to heaven. There's no other feeling in the world like coming into the pregnant pussy of the woman you love and who you know loves you.

Later, we went to bed and she climbed between my legs and gave me the hottest balls and cock suck I'd ever had. As I felt my climax building, I rolled her onto her back, withdrew my cock from between her lovely, sweet lips, and plunged it into her cunt, keeping most of my weight on my extended arms.

I slammed my cock into her—hard, deep, and rough, grinding my hips against hers so she could feel every inch. She must have found my thrusts painful because each time I bottomed out in her, she gasped, shuddered, and bit her lip. But she also clutched at my ass and kept her hips pressed against mine.

"Oh, God, Jake. That hurts. Give me more."

Damn, what a hot fuck that was. I loved every second of being with a woman who could take every inch of my pounding cock without pressing against my hips or shoulders trying to get me to either slow down or take a few inches of cock out.

When the pussy is really good—like it is when you're fucking the only woman you've ever really loved, your cock has a mind of its own. It's determined to totally conquer your lover's pussy. I wasn't the only one in love. My cock was also in love—with her addictive pussy. Being careful not to pound her stomach, I slammed my cock in and out of that sweet, hot, pretty, pink cunt.

She wiggled her ass wildly and fucked at me, her vaginal muscles caressing and loving my cock. Well, I guess her pussy was in love too—with my cock. It felt like a hot, tight glove, reluctant to allow even an inch of cock to be withdrawn from it. She/it made me fight hard to pull out. Each time I did, I slammed back inside that sweet cocoon of pleasure, driving in deep—until she let out this keening noise, raked her nails down my ass, and blew apart under me.

Unable to maintain my weight on my arms any longer, I lowered my stomach onto hers. I gripped her hips, torpedoed my cock deep in her climaxing cunt, and emptied my seed where it rightly belonged—in the pussy of the woman I loved and adored.

After catching my breath, I slid down the bed, parted her legs, and fingered her pussy. Then I opened her slit, slipped my tongue inside, and ate her. I loved the aroma and taste of my cum combined with her natural juices. Delicious. When I'd licked her clean, I lay against her and kissed her, sliding my tongue between her lips.

She must have liked the remnants of us in my kiss, because she curled her fingers in my hair, and devoured my lips and tongue. Within minutes, I eased her onto her stomach, spread her legs wide, and resting my weight on my extended arms, I eased my cock between her lovely, large, dark ass cheeks, and back into that delicious pussy.

Then, conscious that she was pregnant, I rolled us onto our sides, keeping my cock inside her. I cupped a hand over her breasts and closed my eyes while she eagerly fucked herself on my cock until we both came again.

Then, exhausted, but very happy, we finally slept.

Being pregnant made her hornier than ever. How do I know? I woke in the middle of the night to find her climbing onto my erect cock. What could I do? I thrust my cock up her greedy pussy, lay back, and allowed her to shamelessly use me as a fuck object.

She cupped her breasts, closed her eyes, and rode me hard and fast. As she did, she moaned, "Oh, God, Jake, I can't get enough of this sweet, big, hard cock of yours. It feels so good in my pussy."

"Then take it, baby. It's yours. Every hard inch of it."

"Mine." She lifted her hips. "Mine."

"Yours, baby."

"All mine. She slammed her hips down and fucked me until I exploded in her.

She was like that for the next few months—wanting sex nearly every time we were alone. What a life, huh?

I finally discovered Mom was right after all. Beauty is only skin-deep. But love? Well, that goes past the skin straight down to the bone...through it and melts into the marrow until it become a part of your heart and soul. Both of mine are taken by the best thing that's ever happened to me. You might know who I'm talking about Gabrielle Volmer the love of my life, my wife, the mother of my son, and the woman I wouldn't trade for a million bucks.

P. S. For those of you wondering what happened between Lea and Ed, he finally saw the light when Lea's baby was born. In case you're wondering if the baby looked like me or Ed, the answer is neither. He had dark skin. It was clear within moments of his birth that neither Ed nor I was his father.

After weeks of swearing she had no idea how her son looked as biracial as Bree and my son, Jake Junior did, Lea finally admitted she'd had a brief affair with a co-worker. And that's why she'd been desperate to get me to sleep with her, hoping that if she got pregnant while Ed was out of town, the baby would somehow look like one of us. How she thought sleeping with me would help if she were already pregnant by her co-worker is beyond me. I guess it's explained by the fact that Lea isn't the brightest woman on the block.

But then neither was Ed or I, since we were both foolish enough to fall for her. Thankfully we both managed to escape her spell finally.

Anyway, Lea's baby's father sued for his paternal rights and Lea had to let him see his son, something she had not planned to do.

Ed finally had enough and divorced the bitch. Of course she took him for half of what he was worth, but he said it was worth it just to get rid of her. Now he's single again hoping there's another Bree waiting in his future.

As for Jess, she's godmother to our son and she and Bree are great friends these days. But more importantly, she's gotten over that dumb ass Malik. It wasn't easy and at times things looked very bleak for her. Bree and I were really worried about her, but she's finally happy now.

So all is right in my world again. Mom is a happy grandmother with a grandchild she can spoil rotten. Lea is history. Ed and I are close again-as we were before Lea came between us. I'm married to the only woman I've ever loved. She is the woman responsible for changing my life and challenging me to be a much better person than I ever thought I could be. She tells me I'm a good father—which is the highest compliment you can pay a dad.

You're probably thinking we all hate Lea. Well, Ed probably does and maybe Mom does too, but not me and Bree. Don't get me wrong, we don't like her and she sure as hell was not invited to our wedding, but how can we hate her when, for all her bitchy and conniving ways, she was responsible for our meeting?

And she made me face my own shortcomings. No manner the provocation of temptation, I should never have stooped to allowing my cock anywhere near her cunt. I'd done so much more. That was a serious character flaw I have to work on. Still, without her devious plans, I'd never have met and fallen in love with the beautiful woman who wants to give me at least two more kids. Life and the future are looking very good indeed.

The End

Meet Marilyn Lee

Plus you can visit her website to find out more about her and her coming soon books as well:

http://www.marilynlee.org

After her bio you will see her books listed that she has out. Many of her books are both in ebook and print formats.

Marilyn lives, works, and writes on the East Coast of the US. In additional to thoroughly enjoying writing erotic romances in various genres, she enjoys roller-skating, spending time with her large, extended family, and rooting for all her favorite hometown sports teams.

Her other interests include collecting Doc Savage pulp novels from the thirties and forties and collecting Marvel comics from the seventies and eighties (particularly Thor and The Avengers.) Her favorite TV shows are forensic shows, westerns (Gun smoke and Have Gun, Will Travel are particular favorites), and mysteries (Charlie Chan movies in particular).

Her all time favorite mystery movie is probably Dead, Again. She's seen nearly every vampire movie or television show ever made (Forever Knight and Count Yorga, Vampires are favorites. She thoroughly enjoys interacting with readers either through email or via her Yahoo web group.

To subscribe to Marilyn Lee's Love Bytes, <u>marilynlee-subscribe@yahoogroups.com</u>

Red Rose™ Publishing

Summer Storm

Skin Deep

Night Heat

Eye of the Beholder-coming soon

Ellora's s Cave

Bloodlust series:

Bloodlust 5-Midnight Shadows

Conquering Mikhel Dumont

Taming Serge Dumont

Forbidden Desires

Nocturnal Heat

All In The Family

The Talisman

Teacher's Pet

Night of Desires

Trina's Afternoon Delight

Branded

Moonlight Desire

Moonlight Whispers

Road To Rapture

The Fall of Troy

Full Bodied Charmer

Breathless In Black

Playing With Fire

White Christmas

Pleasure Quest

Quest III—Return to Volter

Liquid Silver Books

Yesterday Day's Secret Sins

Changeling Press

Moonlight Healing

Soul Mates

Moonlight Madness Books I & II

Daughters of Takira Series:

One Night in Vegas

Kyla's Awakening

Revelations

Daughters of Takira—complete series

Loose id

Falling For Sharde

Nice Girls Do

Dream Lover

The Dare

Fantasy Knights

By Genre

I/R themes or couples

Teacher's Pet

Moonlight Healing

Night of Desire

Soul Mates

Summer Storm

Bloodlust 5-Midnight Shadows

Trina's Afternoon Delight

Taming Serge Dumont

Forbidden Desires

Nocturnal Heat

All In The Family

The Talisman

Moonlight Desire

Moonlight Whispers

Playing With Fire

White Christmas

Pleasure Quest

Quest III—Return to Volter

Primal Lusts

Moonlight Madness Books I & II

Revelations

A Thing Called Love (also available in paperback)

Falling For Sharde

White Christmas

Where You Find It (written as Mary Lynn)

BBW heroines

Teacher's Pet

Trina's Afternoon Delight

Nice Girls Do

The Fall of Troy

Full Bodied Charmer

Playing With Fire

Falling For Sharde

Bloodlust—Nocturnal Heat

Contemporary settings

Teacher's Pet

Night of Desire

Soul Mates

Trina's Afternoon Delight

The Fall of Troy

Full Bodied Charmer

Playing With Fire

Falling For Sharde

White Christmas

Romantic suspense themes

Yesterday's Secret Sins

A Thing Called Love

Paranormal themes

Moonlight Healing

Soul Mates

Fantasy Knights

Bloodlust 5-Midnight Shadows

Conquering Mikhel Dumont

Taming Serge Dumont

Forbidden Desires

Nocturnal Heat

All In The Family

The Talisman

Moonlight Desire

Moonlight Whispers

Road To Rapture

Pleasure Quest

Quest III—Return to Volter

Branded

Primal Lusts

Moonlight Madness Books I & II

Daughters of Takira Series:

One Night in Vegas

Kyla's Awakening

Revelations

Daughters of Takira—complete series